MIRKA ANDOLFO'S

UNNATURAL

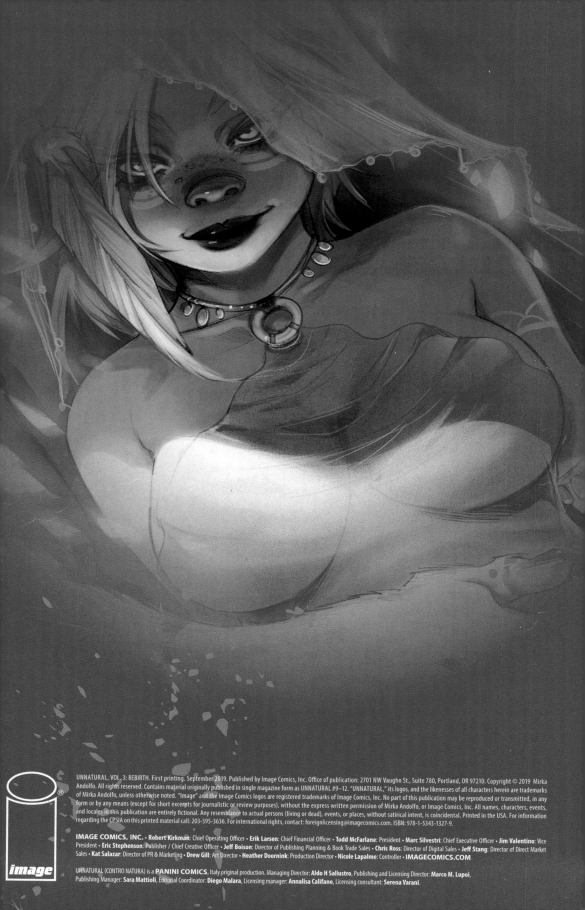

UNNATURAL, VOL. 3: REBIRTH. First printing. September 2019. Published by Image Comics, Inc. Office of publication: 2701 NW Vaughn St., Suite 780, Portland, OR 97210. Copyright © 2019 Mirka Andolfo. All rights reserved. Contains material originally published in single magazine form as UNNATURAL #9–12. "UNNATURAL," its logos, and the likenesses of all characters herein are trademarks of Mirka Andolfo, unless otherwise noted. "Image" and the Image Comics logos are registered trademarks of Image Comics, Inc. No part of this publication may be reproduced or transmitted, in any form or by any means (except for short excerpts for journalistic or review purposes), without the express written permission of Mirka Andolfo, or Image Comics, Inc. All names, characters, events, and locales in this publication are entirely fictional. Any resemblance to actual persons (living or dead), events, or places, without satirical intent, is coincidental. Printed in the USA. For information regarding the CPSIA on this printed material call: 203-595-3636. For international rights, contact: foreignlicensing@imagecomics.com. ISBN: 978-1-5343-1327-9.

UNNATURAL (CONTRO NATURA) is a PANINI COMICS, Italy original production. Managing Director: Aldo H Sallustro, Publishing and Licensing Director: Marco M. Lupoi, Publishing Manager: Sara Mattioli, Editorial Coordinator: Diego Malara, Licensing manager: Annalisa Califano, Licensing consultant: Serena Varani.

PENNY DREADFUL MEETS *DARK SHADOWS*
IN THE NEW GOTH-INSPIRED VICTORIAN MONSTER SERIES
FROM THE BESTSELLING CREATOR OF *UNNATURAL*

MIRKA ANDOLFO'S
MERCY™

image

2020

#GOTMERCY
mirkaandolfo.com

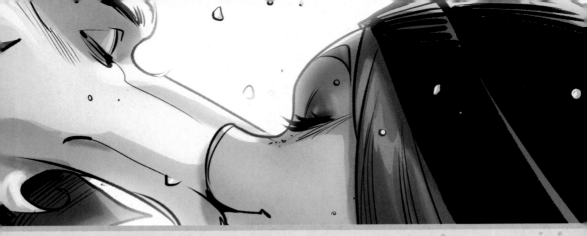

And thanks to Image Comics for making my characters speak English. It's something I've wanted for years, and coming as a completely new author on the US market to the largest independent publisher… Well, I never would've even hoped for it! So, really, thanks to all the Image staff. From that Image Expo in which I was (scared and more timid than ever) hosted alongside so many masters—I never lacked support with their work, availability and sympathy. Cheers!

However, once a door is closed, another one opens… On the following pages there's a little sneak peek (an illustration) of what will come. My next project. And I really hope you'll like it!

A hug and, again…thank you!

MIRKA

PS: As always, you can find me online on social media and my site (finally, really, on the way!).

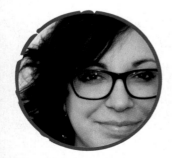

Mirka Andolfo is an Italian creator, working as an artist at DC Comics (*Harley Quinn*, *Wonder Woman*, *DC Bombshells*) and Vertigo (*Hex Wives*). She has drawn comics at Marvel, Dynamite and Aspen Comics. As a creator, *Unnatural* (published so far in Italy, Germany, France, Spain, Poland, Mexico) is her second book, after *Sacro/Profano* (published in Italy, France, Belgium, Netherlands, Spain, Germany and Serbia). You can reach Mirka on her social media channels and on her website: *mirkand.eu*

f mirkand.works   🐦 @Mirkand   📷 @mirkand89

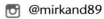

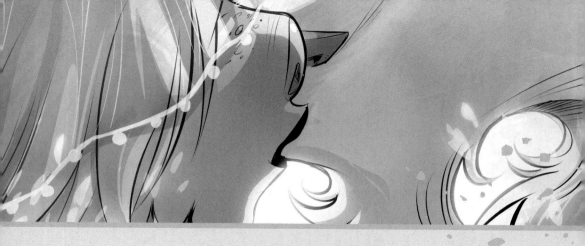

IS THIS THE END?

UNNATURAL HAS COME TO AN END—AS EXPECTED—WITH THE ISSUE THAT YOU HOLD IN YOUR HANDS, NUMBER 12. PERHAPS.

I say "perhaps" because—if you have read the last few pages, you'll already understand—I'm not sure if the misfortunes in Leslie's life end here. At the moment, it's up to you to find an answer to this question… Honestly, I don't know if I'll ever want a concrete answer, so this is a "goodbye" to Leslie and her friends (although it is reluctant). But some small surprises (no, no new comics) should be announced very soon…

I'm very happy with the welcome that this "very peculiar" comic book (Anthropomorphic animals, sensuality, mystery…a little European style, a bit of manga and a little American… It's a very bizarre mix, I'm aware of it!) has received. It has been one of the best and most exhilarating experiences of my life, and it could never have happened without the help of all the people who work with me: starting with the Italian team, the guys at Panini Comics, with whom all this began, Marco Ricompensa and Diego Malara (who still support me on my next adventure, which has just been announced!); Davide G.G. Caci and all Arancia Studio, including the letterer Fabio Amelia and my assistant Gianluca Papi (in turn assisted by Gabriella Sinopoli on the pages of UNNATURAL); all the variant cover artists and finally all the readers who've supported me from the first page to the last one. Thank you so much!

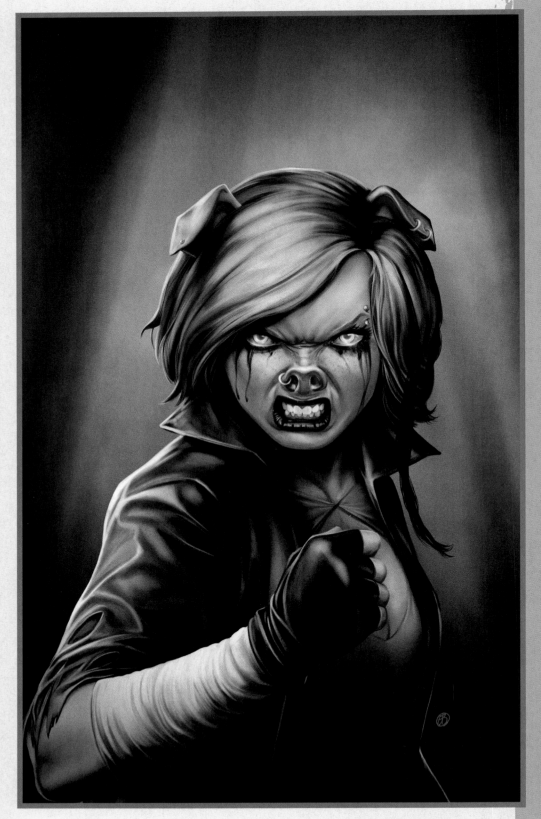

#12 VARIANT BY ELIA BONETTI

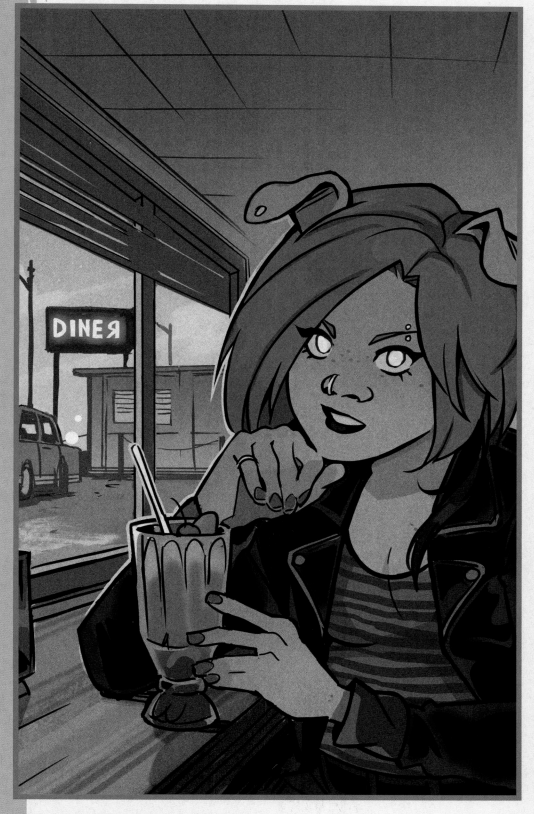

#11 VARIANT BY GABRIEL PICOLO

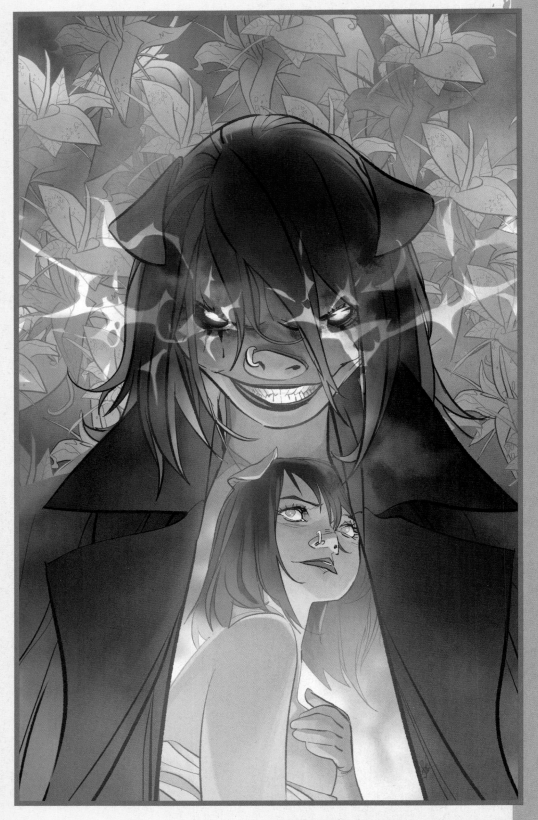

#10 VARIANT BY OTTO SCHMIDT

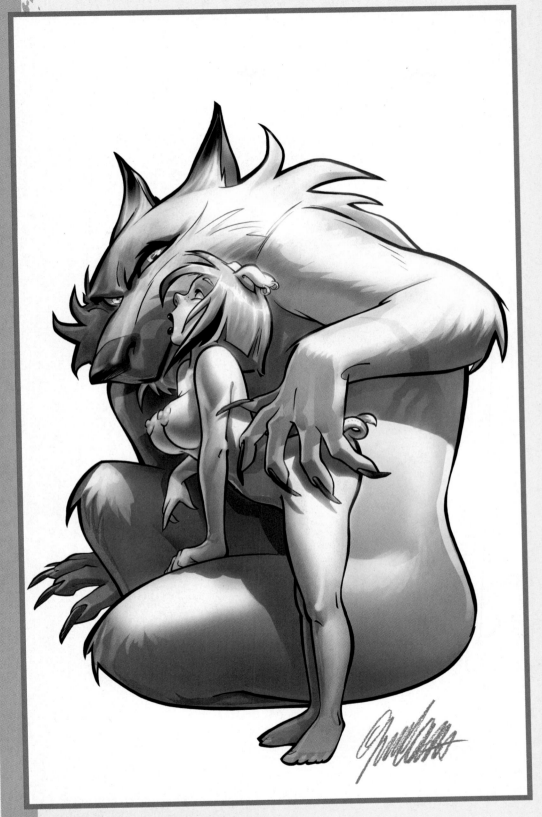

#9 VARIANT BY GIORGIO CAVAZZANO

VARIANT COVERS

2019

EXTRA NATURAL

BUT AS FOR IGNORANCE, WELL...IT'S GOING TO BE A LONG TIME UNTIL WE'RE SAFE FROM THAT.
BUT WE WILL BE. I KNOW IT, EVEN IF IT TAKES TIME. FINALLY...
I'VE GOT HOPE.
FROM NOW ON...
THINGS ARE ONLY GOING TO GET BETTER.
THE END?

NO...NOT FORGIVE HER, KHAL. BUT I DO FEEL SORRY FOR HER. CAROL TOLD ME HOW MUCH THEY MANIPULATED HER TO BRING HER TO THEIR CAUSE. THEY MADE WINSTON DISAPPEAR, THEY ORGANIZED HER MEETING WITH NAPOLEON...
SHE DIED THINKING THE LOVE OF HER LIFE ABANDONED HER, AND EVERY MISGUIDED CHOICE SHE MADE WAS BECAUSE OF THAT... IT'S SAD.
YOU STILL CARE, IN YOUR WAY. YOU'RE STILL SO GOOD...
THAT'S WHY I LOVE YOU!
GNEEK
AND LOOK...YOUR NEW HAIR MATCHES YOUR CHEEKS!
EH, I STILL DON'T KNOW ABOUT THIS COLOR.
SO LET YOUR NATURAL COLOR GROW BACK. WHAT'S THE WORST THAT COULD HAPPEN?
JUST BAD MEMORIES, KHAL...I DON'T WANT TO REMEMBER THE ALBINO, OR THE DREAMS...
THE ONLY THINGS I WANT TO THINK ABOUT ARE THE FRIENDS I'VE LOST...AND THE FUTURE AHEAD. THAT'S IT!
A FUTURE WITH A CHARMING WHITE WOLF, I HOPE?
HE HE! OBVIOUSLY...
I LOVE YOU!
WE'RE SAFE NOW. DON'T FORGET.
DISGUSTING!
AT LEAST SAFE FROM CRAZY CULTS, POLICE WHO'D FRAME YOU AND INSANE ANCIENT SPIRITS WHO'D POSSESS YOU...
DON'T LOOK, JAMES! A BOY SHOULDN'T SEE SUCH UNNATURAL FREAKS!

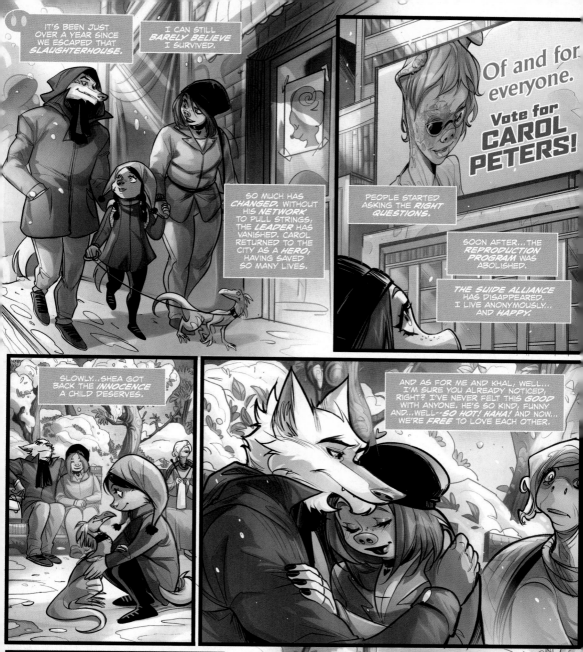

IT'S BEEN JUST OVER A YEAR SINCE WE ESCAPED THAT *SLAUGHTERHOUSE.*

I CAN STILL *BARELY BELIEVE* I SURVIVED.

Of and for everyone.

Vote for CAROL PETERS!

SO MUCH HAS *CHANGED.* WITHOUT HIS *NETWORK* TO PULL STRINGS, THE *LEADER* HAS VANISHED. CAROL RETURNED TO THE CITY AS A *HERO,* HAVING SAVED SO MANY LIVES.

PEOPLE STARTED ASKING THE *RIGHT* QUESTIONS.

SOON AFTER...THE *REPRODUCTION PROGRAM* WAS ABOLISHED.

THE SLIDE ALLIANCE HAS DISAPPEARED. I LIVE ANONYMOUSLY... AND *HAPPY.*

SLOWLY...SHEA GOT BACK THE *INNOCENCE* A CHILD DESERVES.

AND AS FOR ME AND KHAL, WELL... I'M SURE YOU ALREADY NOTICED, RIGHT? I'VE NEVER FELT THIS *GOOD* WITH ANYONE. HE'S SO KIND, FUNNY AND...WELL--*SO HOT!* HAHA! AND NOW... WE'RE *FREE* TO LOVE EACH OTHER.

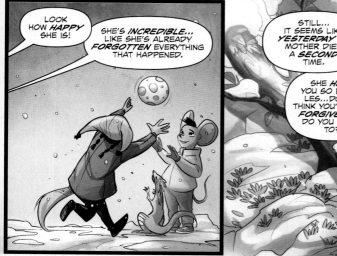

LOOK HOW *HAPPY* SHE IS!

SHE'S *INCREDIBLE...* LIKE SHE'S ALREADY *FORGOTTEN* EVERYTHING THAT HAPPENED.

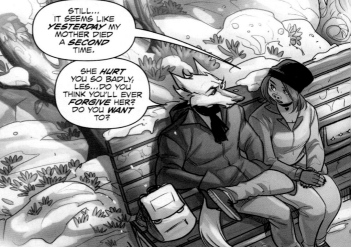

STILL... IT SEEMS LIKE *YESTERDAY* MY MOTHER DIED A *SECOND* TIME.

SHE *HURT* YOU SO BADLY, LES...DO YOU THINK YOU'LL EVER *FORGIVE* HER? DO YOU *WANT* TO?

FIRST THEY CANCEL THE REPRODUCTION PROGRAM...NOW THIS?
DAMN CAROL... SHE WON'T STOP UNTIL WE LOSE EVERYTHING, WILL SHE?
NEW ROARK TIMES
CLOSES THE TERRIBLE "SLAUGHTERHOUSE"
"The atrocities that were committed in that building are not worthy of a people that is defined as civil."
The first words of New Roark's new major, CAROL PETERS.
VIRGIL! ARE YOU MONOLOGUING WHILE YOU READ THE NEWS AGAIN?
AH! MR. HANS!
GET BACK TO WORK! I DON'T PAY YOU TO STAND IN THE STREET!
B-BUT... I'M ON BREAK!
YOUR BREAK ENDED EIGHT SECONDS AGO!
O-OH, I'M SORRY, SIR!
COME TO TRY OUR NEW GINSENGCINO!
!
THAT'S... IT CAN'T BE. THAT GIRL...
HAVEN'T I SEEN HER BEFORE?
GRRR!

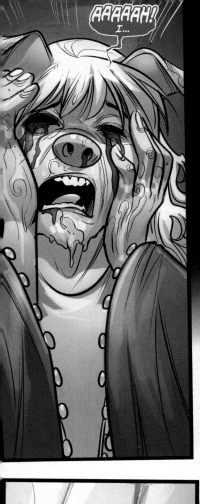

AAAAAH! I...

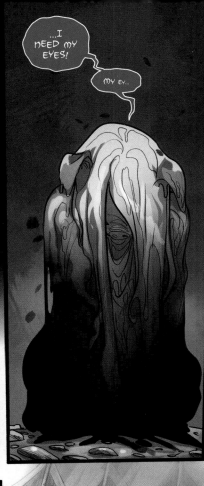

...I NEED MY EYES!

MY EY...

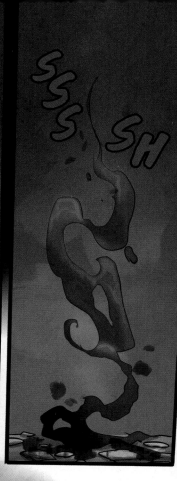

SSSSH

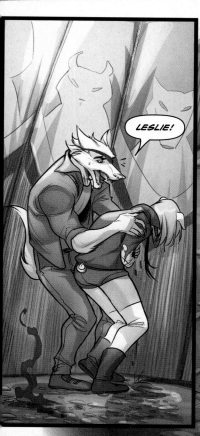

LESLIE!

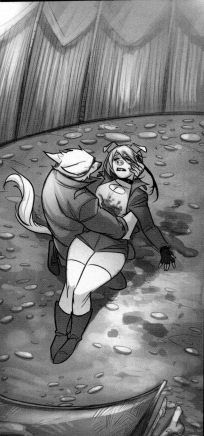

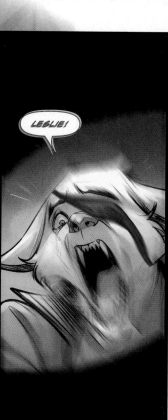

LESLIE!

ALL IT MEANS IS THAT I'LL HAVE TO GET MY HANDS DIRTY TO FINISH YOU OFF.
STHUUM
IN HIS MADNESS, THE ALBINO'S FORGOTTEN THAT I KNOW HOW HIS POWER WORKS.
THE EYES.
TO STOP YOU FROM USING YOUR POWER!
NOOOOOO!

THE ALBINO'S TOO STRONG. BUT MY MOTHER'S NOT.
NONE CAN OPPOSE ME! LEAST OF ALL YOU, GIRL!
UUUGH
IF HER BODY WAS TRULY STRONG ENOUGH TO CONTAIN THE ALBINO, HE'D HAVE KILLED ME ALREADY.
WHAT DO YOU THINK WILL HAPPEN FIRST?
WILL YOUR HEAD EXPLODE? OR WILL YOUR NECK SNAP?
I-I... AAAAH!
NEXT? I--I'LL USE THE LAST OF MY STRENGTH...
FOR WHAT?
TO...TO STOP YOU...
THE FULCRUM OF THE ALBINO'S POWER IS ALSO HIS ONLY WEAK POINT.

NGAH!
=UGH=
YOU...YOU RESIST ME...
HOW?!
YOUR HEAD SHOULD BE EXPLODING!
YEAH, MY HEAD HURTS... BUT YOU KNOW WHAT?
I'M STILL HERE! AND I'M GOING TO STOP YOU, YOU BASTARD!
IT...MAYBE IT WON'T WORK... BUT THIS IS MY ONLY CHANCE!

I--I CAN'T...THE ALBINO...
I CAN'T CONTROL HIM. HE'S TOO STRONG...
HELLO, MY BRIDE!
YOU FOUGHT ME FOR SO LONG, DISRESPECTED MY WILL, AND NOW THAT I DON'T NEED YOUR BODY...
IT'S TIME TO DIE!
HHHNNNG...

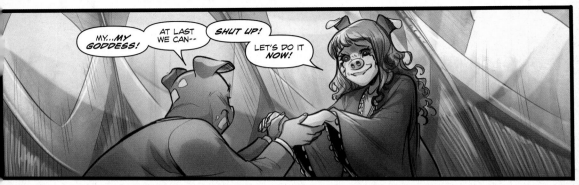

MY...MY GODDESS!

AT LAST WE CAN--

SHUT UP!

LET'S DO IT NOW!

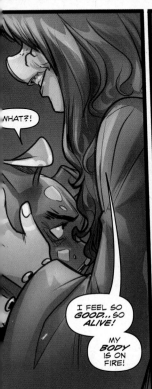

WHAT?!

I FEEL SO GOOD...SO ALIVE!

MY BODY IS ON FIRE!

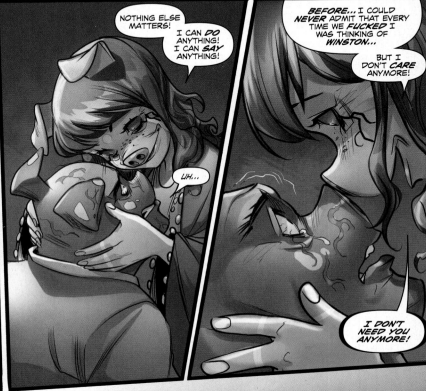

NOTHING ELSE MATTERS! I CAN DO ANYTHING! I CAN SAY ANYTHING!

UH...

BEFORE...I COULD NEVER ADMIT THAT EVERY TIME WE FUCKED I WAS THINKING OF WINSTON...

BUT I DON'T CARE ANYMORE!

I DON'T NEED YOU ANYMORE!

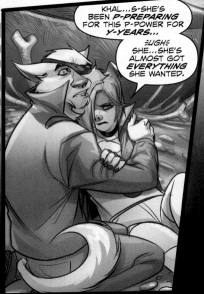

KHAL...S-SHE'S BEEN P-PREPARING FOR THIS P-POWER FOR Y-YEARS...

≥UGH≤ SHE...SHE'S ALMOST GOT EVERYTHING SHE WANTED.

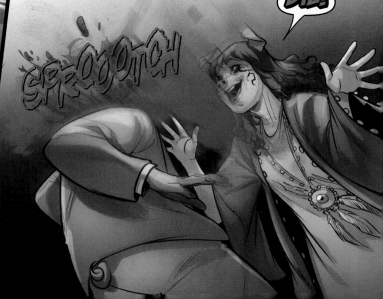

DIE!

SPROOOTCH

YES! *YES!*
COME TO ME, ALBINO! *COME!*
STUPID GIRL... HIS POWER WAS *WASTED* ON YOU.
ONLY *I* CAN *HONOR* IT, *AMPLIFY* IT TO EVEN *GREATER* HEIGHTS!
THE *MIGHT*, THE *STRENGTH*... IT'S *BEAUTIFUL!*
NO, LESLIE...
YOU... YOU FINALLY *DID* IT, MAXIME!
YOU CAN'T *DIE* HERE, LIKE THIS...
PLEASE!
KHAL...

NOOOOO!
MAXIME!
H-HOW COULD YOU?
SOMEONE HAD TO.
LESLIE...
IT WASN'T FOR YOU TO DECIDE!
MY...MY LITTLE GIRL...I'M SO... SO SORRY...
STAY CLOSE, PLEASE...YOU HAVE TO KNOW...I DIDN'T WANT IT TO END LIKE THIS, I DIDN'T...
I'M NOT LIKE YOU, YOU KNOW? I'M NOT BES...
BUT BES COULD ONLY DO WHAT SHE DID WITH THE HELP OF A SHAMAN...
AND I'M A SHAMAN.
SHAMANS ARE THE ONLY ONES WHO CAN CREATE SACRED WEAPONS...THERE'S NO ONE ELSE.
AND THOSE WEAPONS... ARE FORGED IN BLOOD!

DON'T TOUCH HIM!
NO, MAXIME! DON'T MIND ME...
STOP, KHAL! I CAN DO THIS ALONE!
BUT YOU CAN'T, LES...
BECAUSE YOU'RE GOOD!
IF YOU KILLED YOUR MOTHER, YOU'D NEVER FORGIVE YOURSELF...
BUT ME?
I'LL DO IT GLADLY!
STRAAATCH
MOM!

YOU HIT SO WEAK! WHY?
YOU'RE HOLDING BACK... IS IT BECAUSE I'M YOUR MOTHER?
YOU SHOULD KNOW, LESLIE... MY STRENGTH ISN'T JUST SPIRITUAL. JUST LIKE YOUR FURRY FRIEND KHAL...
I KILL WITH MY BARE HANDS!
AAAH!
COME ON! YOU'RE NOT EVEN TRYING TO STOP ME! I THOUGHT YOU WERE TOUGH!
=GHHH=
I CAN'T BELIEVE IT.
JONES WAS RIGHT!
I HATE HER WITH EVERY FIBER OF MY BEING...BUT I'M STILL HOLDING BACK! I CAN'T KEEP THIS UP!
=GHHH=
STOP,
OR THIS LITTLE PIG IS DEAD!
!
=GHHH=
I CAN CRUSH HIS SKULL LIKE GLASS! OR OPEN HIS THROAT...
YOUR CHOICE.

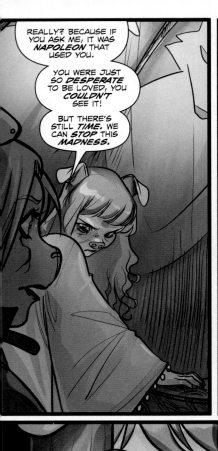

REALLY? BECAUSE IF YOU ASK ME, IT WAS *NAPOLEON* THAT USED YOU.

YOU WERE JUST SO *DESPERATE* TO BE LOVED, YOU *COULDN'T* SEE IT!

BUT THERE'S STILL *TIME*. WE CAN *STOP* THIS *MADNESS*.

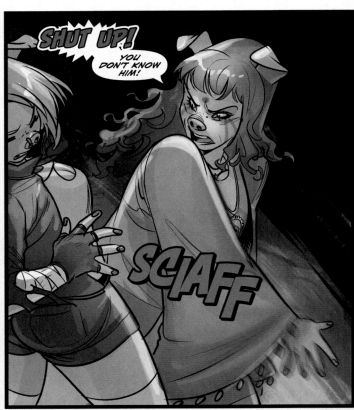

SHUT UP!

YOU *DON'T KNOW* HIM!

SCIAFF

YOU'RE NOTHING BUT A *PERVERT* AND A *LIAR*.

YOU'RE *NOTHING* LIKE ME!

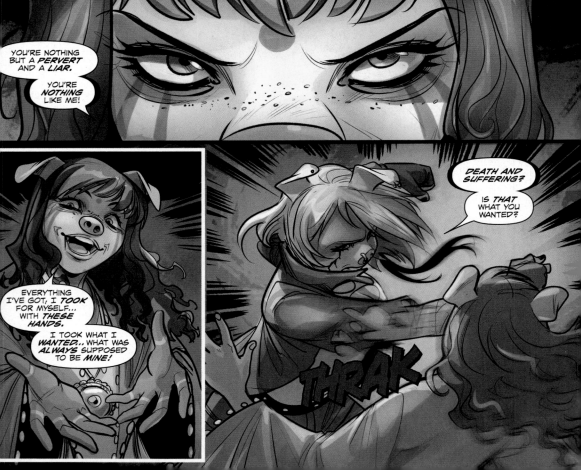

EVERYTHING I'VE GOT, I *TOOK* FOR MYSELF... WITH *THESE* HANDS.

I TOOK WHAT I *WANTED*... WHAT WAS *ALWAYS* SUPPOSED TO BE *MINE!*

DEATH AND SUFFERING?

IS *THAT* WHAT YOU WANTED?

THRAK

YOU KNOW... AFTER I BECAME THE SHAMAN, I MADE THIS PLACE MY SANCTUARY.
A PLACE WHERE, UNLIKE IN MY OLD LIFE... PEOPLE RESPECTED ME.
I COULD ALMOST SAY THEY DIDN'T JUST RESPECT ME... THEY WORSHIPED ME.
MY BLOOD WAS ESSENTIAL FOR THE RITUAL.
WHY ARE YOU DOING ALL THIS?
WHAT'S THE POINT IN AWAKENING A MONSTER THAT COULD KILL EVERYONE IN THE WORLD... INCLUDING YOU?
HE WON'T. YOU'RE WRONG. I'M SPIRITUALLY READY.
I'LL TAKE THE ALBINO INTO MYSELF.
AFTER THAT, MY POWER WILL BE NEARLY LIMITLESS.
YOUR CHILDISH REACTION TO WHAT JONES DID TO YOU... THAT'LL SEEM LIKE A PLAYGROUND SPAT COMPARED TO WHAT I'LL DO.
THE WORLD WILL FINALLY BE IN THE HANDS OF THE SUPERIOR RACE, THANKS TO THE ALLIANCE!
THANKS TO OUR NETWORK OF SURVEILLANCE CAMERAS... I'LL BE ABLE TO REACH EVERY LIVING SOUL IN THE CITY!
AND THAT'S JUST THE BEGINNING...
THAT PUPPET OF A KOALA WILL HELP ME CREATE REAL GHETTOS! FINALLY, THE UNWORTHY WILL BE SEPARATED FROM THEIR MASTERS!
BUT... HOW CAN YOU TALK LIKE THAT?
THAT LION DIDN'T MEAN ANYTHING TO YOU?
THE REPRODUCTION PROGRAM RUINED YOUR LIFE!
YOUR FATHER WASN'T THE RIGHT MAN FOR ME.
THE PROGRAM WORKS, BUT IT'S NOT PERFECT.
WINSTON WASN'T RIGHT, HE JUST TOOK ADVANTAGE OF ME WHILE I WAS VULNERABLE.
HE USED ME!
BUT NAPOLEON... HE SAVED ME FROM MYSELF.
HE'S THE ONLY ONE WHO WAS HONEST WITH ME.
HE HELPED ME UNDERSTAND MY TRUE ORIGINS.
HE SHOWED ME HOW MUCH WE COULD DO TOGETHER... SHOWED ME MY DESTINY!

"SHE SAID SHE HAD TO CALL OFF THE ALBINO."
YOU CAN'T STOP IT, YOU STUPID GIRL! SOON I'LL BE FREE!
I DON'T CARE! YOU'RE NOT FREE YET! AND UNTIL THEN...
SHUT THE HELL UP!
IF YOU WISH...
BUT SOMEONE SHOULD TELL YOU YOUR MOTHER WANTS YOU TO CHASE HER.
I CAN FEEL IT...
SHE'S LEADING YOU SOMEWHERE VERY SPECIAL.
AS FAR AS I'M CONCERNED, SHE CAN GO STRAIGHT TO HELL.
AS USUAL, YOU'RE NAÏVE. YOU DON'T UNDERSTAND...
THIS PLACE IS DANGEROUS!
DO NOT GO IN!
THIS PLACE...
?
...I'VE SEEN IT BEFORE!

UNNATURAL™

VOLUME THREE · REBIRTH

writer, artist and colorist
MIRKA ANDOLFO

colors assistant
GIANLUCA PAPI
(ARANCIA STUDIO)

lettering and production
FABIO AMELIA
(ARANCIA STUDIO)

translation from italian
ARANCIA STUDIO

cover artist
MIRKA ANDOLFO

editors
DIEGO MALARA
MARCO RICOMPENSA

design
ALESSANDRO GUCCIARDO
FABIO AMELIA

CHAPTER NINE

New Roark.
"LISTEN DORY, IT'S NOT MY FAULT I'VE GOT A DEMANDING JOB...
GOTH LOL
"YOU THINK I LIKE TO WORK LATE?
GOTH LOL
"SEE? THAT'S WHAT I'M SAYING! I LOVE YOU!
"OF COURSE I DO!
"WHAT? YES, WHY WOULDN'T I BE? I PROMISE, HON. I'M STILL FOLLOWING MY DIET."
VEG MENU
WHOOPS! THERE'S A CUSTOMER! GOTTA GO! LOVE YOU!
KISSES!
CLICK
SALES
SUFF
FINALLY!

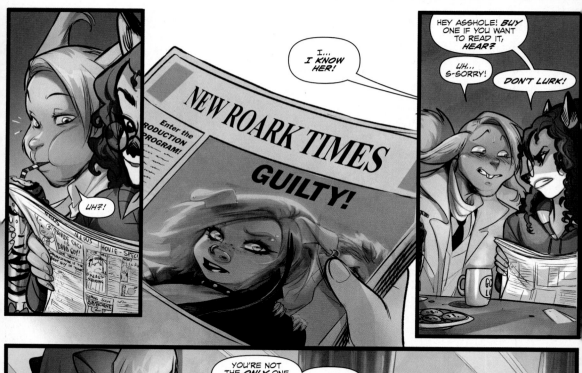

I.... I KNOW HER!

UH?!

NEW ROARK TIMES

Enter the PRODUCTION PROGRAM!

GUILTY!

HEY ASSHOLE! *BUY* ONE IF YOU WANT TO READ IT, *HEAR?*

UH... S-SORRY!

DON'T LURK!

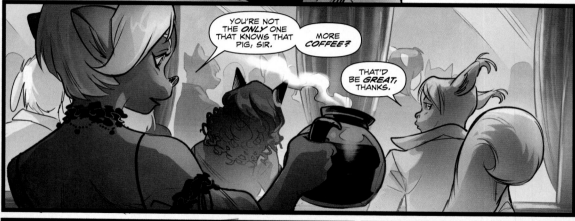

YOU'RE NOT THE *ONLY* ONE THAT KNOWS THAT PIG, SIR.

MORE *COFFEE?*

THAT'D BE *GREAT,* THANKS.

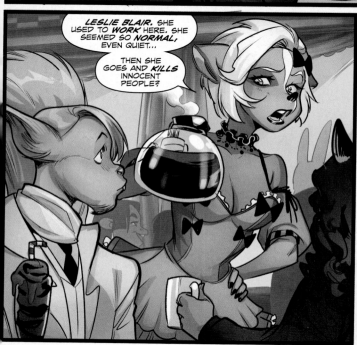

LESLIE BLAIR. SHE USED TO *WORK* HERE. SHE SEEMED SO *NORMAL,* EVEN QUIET...

THEN SHE GOES AND *KILLS* INNOCENT PEOPLE?

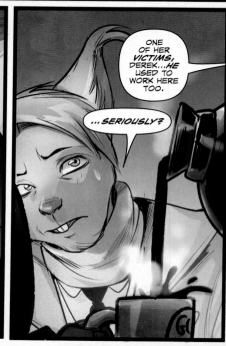

ONE OF HER *VICTIMS,* DEREK...HE USED TO WORK HERE TOO.

...*SERIOUSLY?*

HOW DO YOU KNOW LESLIE? WERE YOU FRIENDS?
I NEVER SAW YOU AROUND HERE.
NO, NO. I MET HER ONCE.
I WAS HER TUTOR FOR THE REPRODUCTION PROGRAM.
HONESTLY... I DON'T BELIEVE IT. HER? A MURDERER? SHE WAS SO INSECURE...
A WIMP, EVEN. ANNOYING. TRIVIAL. INDECISIVE. AND THAT BLUE HAIR...
NO, I DIDN'T KNOW HER WELL, BUT I NEVER WOULD'VE PEGGED HER FOR A KILLER.
I'D PEGGED HER FOR SOMETHING, THAT'S FOR SURE.
THE ONLY ONE SHE EVER TALKED TO WAS DEREK... HIM AND THAT TATTOOED MOUSE THAT WOULD VISIT SOMETIMES. I THINK LESLIE LIVED WITH HER.
WORD WAS THEY WERE LOVERS. LESLIE WAS ONE OF THOSE DEGENERATES.
REAL TALK? I HOPE SHE'S GONE. I'D FEEL SAFER WITHOUT HER KIND AROUND.
NEW ROARK TIMES
Enter the REPRODUCTION PROGRAM!
GUILTY!
GONE? I WONDER... WHO KNOWS WHERE SHE IS NOW, OR WHAT SHE'S DOING...
AGAIN?!
EHM...

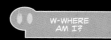

W-WHERE AM I?

WHAT'S HAPPENING?

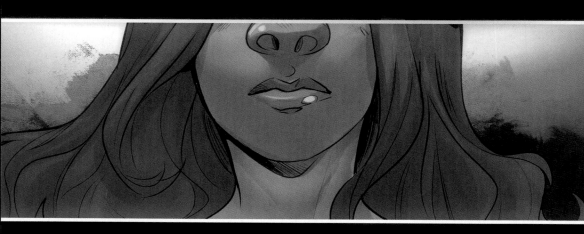

IS THAT...*MOM?*

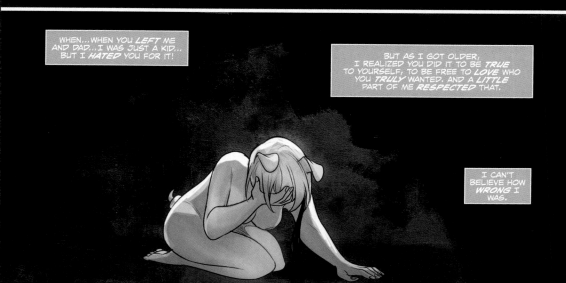

WHEN...WHEN YOU *LEFT* ME AND DAD...I WAS JUST A KID... BUT I *HATED* YOU FOR IT!

BUT AS I GOT OLDER, I REALIZED YOU DID IT TO BE *TRUE* TO YOURSELF, TO BE FREE TO *LOVE* WHO YOU *TRULY* WANTED. AND A *LITTLE* PART OF ME *RESPECTED* THAT.

I CAN'T BELIEVE HOW *WRONG* I WAS.

FOOL! RESPECT? YOU SHOULD BE FAR MORE GRATEFUL TO YOUR MOTHER.
IT'S TRUE, AS "THE GLANCE," SHE WISHES TO MANIPULATE US.
BUT SHE'S ALSO THE REASON WE'RE FINALLY HERE, NOW...
TOGETHER.
YOUR BODY... YOUR SPIRIT... IS ONE WITH MINE.
IS IT NOT WONDERFUL, MY BRIDE?
NO!

STOP!
NO!
IF I STAY HERE...
YOU'LL KILL THEM!
LESLIEEEEE!
IT'S HOPELESS TO RUN, BRIDE. I'VE NEVER BEEN SO CLOSE TO FULLY AWAKENING.
THERE'S NOWHERE TO GO, THERE'S NO ESCAPE...

IT'S JUST A MATTER OF TIME BEFORE MY COMPLETE AWAKENING...
AGH!
KHAL! WE'VE GOT TO DO SOMETHING FOR THAT WOUND! YOU CAN'T MAKE IT MUCH FARTHER--
GET AWAY FROM ME!
THIS IS YOUR DAMN FAULT, SAYA!
MY FAULT...
I WAS WRONG, OKAY? BUT I WAS TRYING TO SAVE CAROL!
THE SAME CAROL THAT SAID WE WERE ALL EXPENDABLE?
BUT YOU'VE-- YOU'VE SEEN WHAT LESLIE IS! WHAT SHE'S BECOME! SHE'S DANGEROUS! SHE'S A THREAT TO EVERYBODY!

IT'S LIKE CAROL SAID, KHAL. WE'RE ALL EXPENDABLE...
...
THROOOOOM
"...EVEN LESLIE."
CALM DOWN, MISTER NAPOLEON, SIR!
WE KNOW IT'S HARD...
NO!
CRASH
YOU DON'T KNOW SHIT!
YOU DON'T KNOW ANYTHING!
TUMP
S-SIR...

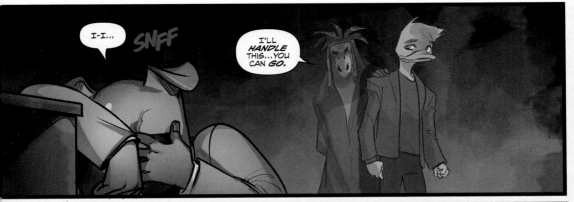

I-I...

SNFF

I'LL *HANDLE* THIS...YOU CAN *GO.*

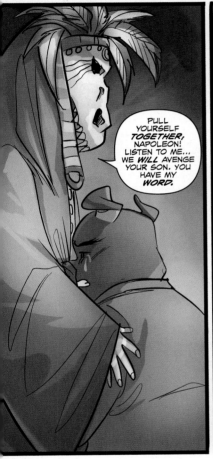

PULL YOURSELF *TOGETHER,* NAPOLEON! LISTEN TO ME... WE *WILL* AVENGE YOUR SON. YOU HAVE MY *WORD.*

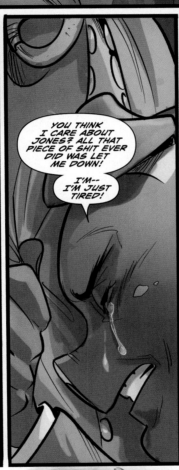

YOU THINK I CARE ABOUT *JONES?* ALL THAT PIECE OF SHIT EVER DID WAS LET ME *DOWN!*

I'M-- I'M JUST *TIRED!*

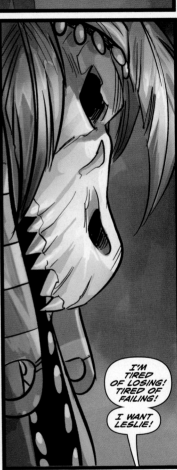

I'M *TIRED* OF *LOSING!* TIRED OF *FAILING!*

I WANT *LESLIE!*

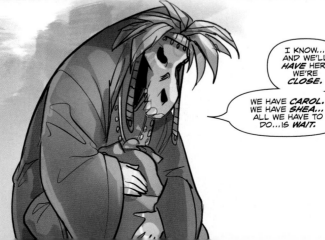

I *KNOW...* AND WE'LL *HAVE* HER. WE'RE *CLOSE.*

WE HAVE *CAROL.* WE HAVE *SHEA...* ALL WE HAVE TO DO...IS *WAIT.*

"I LEFT CAROL TO THE WISE CARE OF LUCREZIA.
"SHE'S DOING HER BEST TO KEEP HER DOCILE.
AAAAH!
TAP
"WE CAN'T AFFORD FOR CAROL TO BECOME LUCID AGAIN... THAT'S HOW PROBLEMS START."
"WHAT ABOUT THE BRAT?"
"SHE'S WITH THE OTHER KIDS."
"SHOULDN'T WE ISOLATE HER TOO?"
"WE'RE WATCHING HER. BUT THIS RAISES FEWER QUESTIONS."
GOOD MORNING, LITTLE ONES!
YOU'VE ALL GOT SUCH LONG FACES!
THEN AGAIN... I'D BE SAD TOO, IF I WERE YOU.
YOUR PARENTS ARE UNNATURAL SCUM... HOMOSEXUALS, INTERSPECIES DEVIANTS. THEY'RE SICK!
THEIR DEGENERATE RELATIONSHIPS BETRAY THE SACREDNESS OF NATURE, THEY PERVERT THE DEFINITION OF FAMILY.
YOU'RE HERE BECAUSE OF THEM.

MY DAD DIDN'T DO ANYTHING WRONG!
I WANT TO GO HOME!
YOU'LL NEVER SEE THAT PERVERT AGAIN!
DON'T YOU GET IT? YOU'RE SICK TOO!
THAT FAGGOT POISONED YOUR MIND! HE RUINED YOUR LIFE!
TCHAK
YOU'RE ALL HERE BECAUSE YOU'RE INFECTED! NO EXCEPTIONS!
THE WORLD NEEDS NORMAL, HEALTHY ADULTS READY TO HAVE NORMAL, HEALTHY CHILDREN! THAT IS THE FUTURE OF EACH SPECIES!
OTHERWISE, THE PRICE OF THIS PERVERT LOVE... IS EXTINCTION.
THE REPRODUCTION PROGRAM ALONE IS NOT ENOUGH.
YOUR PARENTS PUT YOU KIDS IN DANGER, BUT THERE'S STILL TIME TO SAVE YOU. YOU'RE STILL YOUNG...

"YOU CAN STILL LEARN WHAT'S NATURAL."
HI LITTLE GUY!
HI HI HI!
YOU SHOULDN'T SMOKE IN THE HOUSE.
AT LEAST GO TO THE GARDEN.
AND YOU SHOULDN'T GET DRUNK IN FRONT OF YOUR DAUGHTER.
BUT DON'T WORRY...
SOMEHOW I THINK YOUR "PARENT OF THE YEAR" AWARD'S STILL ON ITS WAY.
AAAH!
SHUT YOUR MOUTH!
DISRESPECTFUL BITCH!
THUMP
I-I...CAN'T STAND THIS ANYMORE, PHIL...
YOU SAID IF WE HAD A KID... IT WOULD GET BETTER FOR BOTH OF US!
THIS IS BETTER? YOU GET EVERYTHING YOU WANT WHILE I WORK MY ASS OFF EVERY DAMN DAY?
MOMMY? DADDY? WHAT'S THAT NOISE?
NOTHING, MY LOVE!
YOUR MOM JUST SLIPPED. SHE'S CLUMSY. EVERYTHING'S FINE!
REALLY? AGAIN?
SHE'S REALLY DISTRACTED, RIGHT?
HA! SHE'S SO SILLY!
"SILLY, RIGHT...

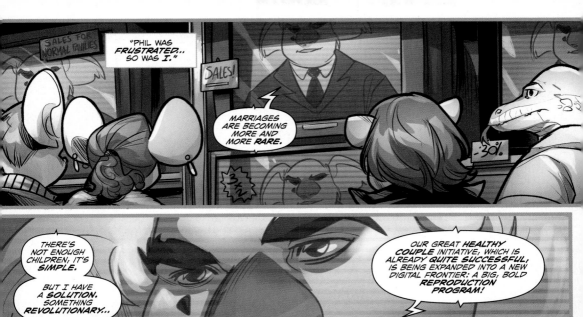

"PHIL WAS *FRUSTRATED...* SO WAS *I.*"

SALES FOR NORMAL FAMILIES

SALES!

MARRIAGES ARE BECOMING MORE AND MORE *RARE.*

-30%

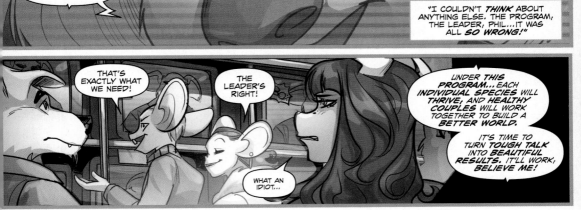

THERE'S NOT ENOUGH CHILDREN; IT'S *SIMPLE.*

BUT I HAVE A *SOLUTION.* SOMETHING *REVOLUTIONARY...*

OUR GREAT *HEALTHY COUPLE* INITIATIVE, WHICH IS ALREADY *QUITE SUCCESSFUL,* IS BEING EXPANDED INTO A NEW DIGITAL FRONTIER: A BIG, BOLD *REPRODUCTION PROGRAM!*

"I COULDN'T *THINK* ABOUT ANYTHING ELSE. THE PROGRAM, THE LEADER, PHIL....IT WAS ALL *SO WRONG!*"

THAT'S EXACTLY WHAT WE NEED!

THE LEADER'S RIGHT!

WHAT AN IDIOT...

UNDER THIS *PROGRAM...* EACH *INDIVIDUAL SPECIES* WILL *THRIVE,* AND *HEALTHY COUPLES* WILL WORK TOGETHER TO BUILD A *BETTER WORLD.*

IT'S TIME TO TURN *TOUGH TALK* INTO *BEAUTIFUL RESULTS.* IT'LL WORK, BELIEVE ME!

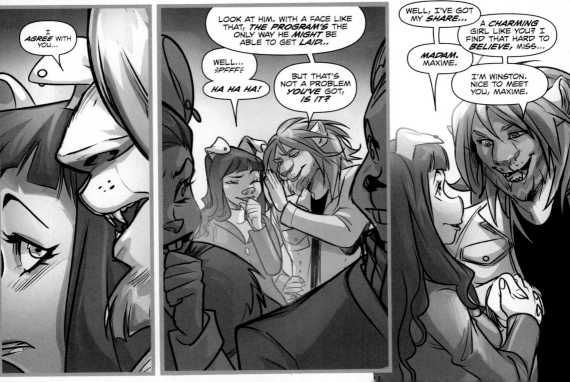

I *AGREE* WITH YOU...

LOOK AT HIM. WITH A FACE LIKE THAT, *THE PROGRAM'S* THE ONLY WAY HE *MIGHT* BE ABLE TO GET *LAID...*

WELL... ≥PFFF≤

HA HA HA!

BUT THAT'S NOT A PROBLEM *YOU'VE* GOT, IS IT?

WELL, I'VE GOT MY *SHARE...*

A *CHARMING* GIRL LIKE YOU? I FIND THAT HARD TO *BELIEVE,* MISS...

MADAM. MAXIME.

I'M WINSTON. NICE TO MEET YOU, MAXIME.

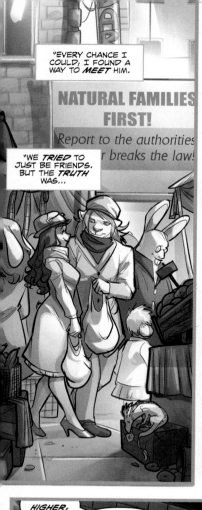

"EVERY CHANCE I COULD, I FOUND A WAY TO *MEET* HIM.

NATURAL FAMILIES FIRST!

Report to the authorities r breaks the law!

"WE *TRIED* TO JUST BE FRIENDS. BUT THE *TRUTH* WAS...

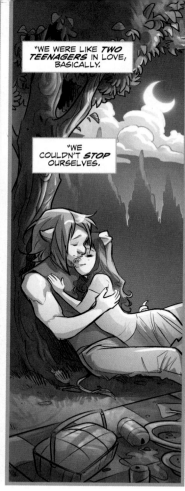

"WE WERE LIKE *TWO TEENAGERS* IN LOVE, BASICALLY.

"WE COULDN'T *STOP* OURSELVES.

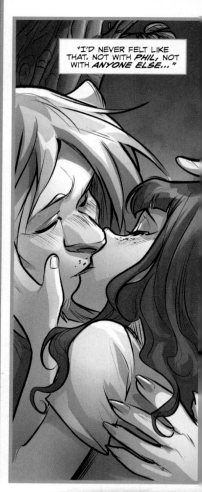

"I'D NEVER FELT LIKE THAT. NOT WITH *PHIL*, NOT WITH *ANYONE ELSE*..."

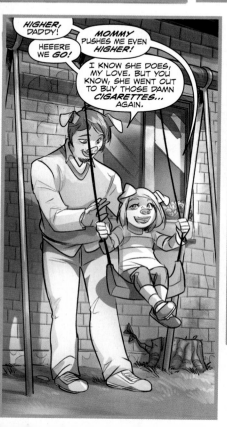

HIGHER, DADDY!

HEEERE WE GO!

MOMMY PUSHES ME EVEN HIGHER!

I KNOW SHE DOES, MY LOVE. BUT YOU KNOW, SHE WENT OUT TO BUY THOSE DAMN *CIGARETTES*... AGAIN.

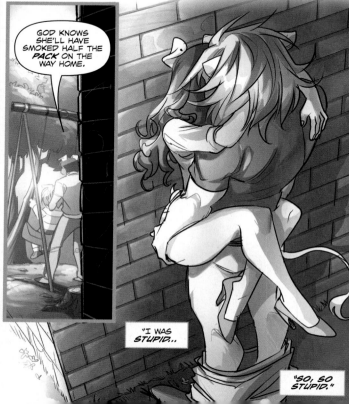

GOD KNOWS SHE'LL HAVE SMOKED HALF THE *PACK* ON THE WAY HOME.

"I WAS *STUPID*...

"SO, SO *STUPID*."

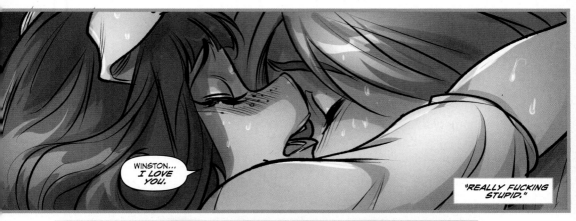

WINSTON... I LOVE YOU.

"REALLY FUCKING STUPID."

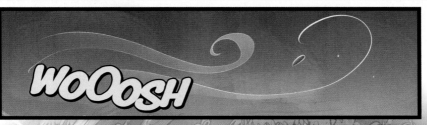

WOOOSH

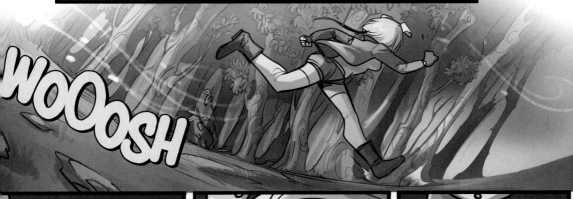

WOOOSH

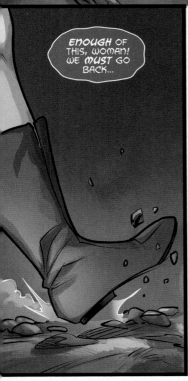

ENOUGH OF THIS, WOMAN! WE MUST GO BACK...

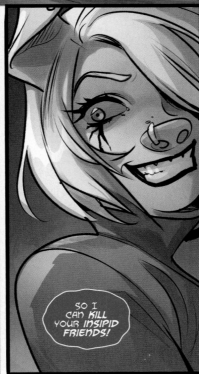

SO I CAN KILL YOUR INSIPID FRIENDS!

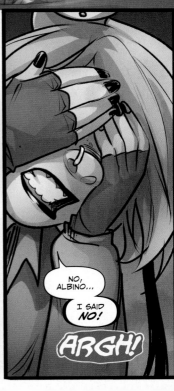

NO, ALBINO... I SAID NO!

ARGH!

STOP THIS, GIRL!
HOW CAN YOU STILL RESIST?
YOUR BODY IS MINE!
GIVE IN! ACCEPT IT!

NO! YOU...
DID ALL THIS
TO ME...
NOW IT'S MY TURN...
I'M FINALLY TAKING MY
LIFE INTO MY OWN HANDS.

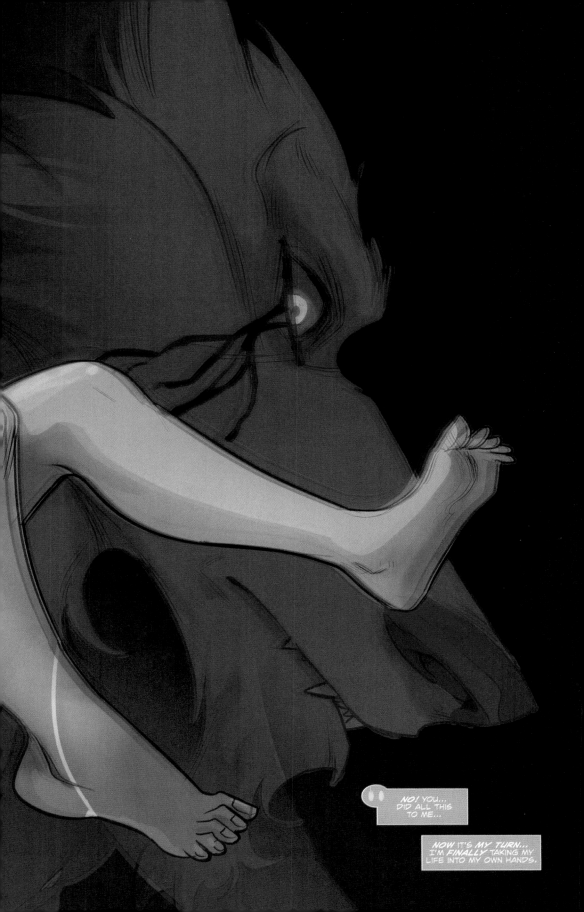

PLEASE. I'VE BEEN IN YOUR HEAD...AND YOUR HEART.
I KNOW HOW YOU FEEL.
GIVE IN TO IT, MY LOVE...
REMEMBER...
REMEMBER YOUR LIFE AS BES...
I CAN'T DENY IT.
IT'S NO TRICK. I DO FEEL SOMETHING FOR HIM, DESPITE EVERYTHING, DESPITE HIM BEING A MONSTER.
HE'S...HE'S MAKING ME HIS. COMPLETELY.
AND I THINK... I'M LETTING HIM. I WANT IT, WANT THIS.

THERE SHE IS! COME ON!
AAAAAAH!
LESLIE! CAN--CAN YOU HEAR ME?
ARE YOU OKAY?
YOU'RE RIGHT. I USED TO LOVE YOU.
I LOVED YOU DEEPLY. THERE'S MORE THAN HATE AND DARKNESS INSIDE YOU.
"THERE ARE PLEASANT MEMORIES OF US, JUST BEFORE I DIED...
"BUT YOU'RE THE ONE THAT RUINED EVERYTHING."
I WAS BORN IN HATRED AND I FEED ON FEAR AND PAIN.
IT'S MY NATURE.
NATURE DOESN'T MATTER! YOU CAN BE ANYTHING YOU WANT, I KNOW YOU CAN! WE'RE ONE NOW, I'M IN YOUR HEAD AND HEART TOO...TRY TO REMEMBER!
I...DON'T THINK THERE'S ANYTHING TO BE DONE, NOT NOW...IT'S FAR TOO LATE...
IT'S NOT! YOU'VE STILL GOT TIME--WE'VE GOT TIME!
YOU... TRULY BELIEVE THAT?
YES! I DO!

THEN THERE'S... JUST ONE PROBLEM.
WHAT?
I DON'T WANT TO CHANGE!
?
IF... THAT'S TRUE, ALBINO...
THEN EVEN IF I FAILED BEFORE...
THIS TIME, THERE REALLY IS ONLY ONE SOLUTION...
TUMP
FOR US BOTH.

CHAPTER
TEN

GLUB
GLUB
?
GLUB
GLUB
!
GLUB

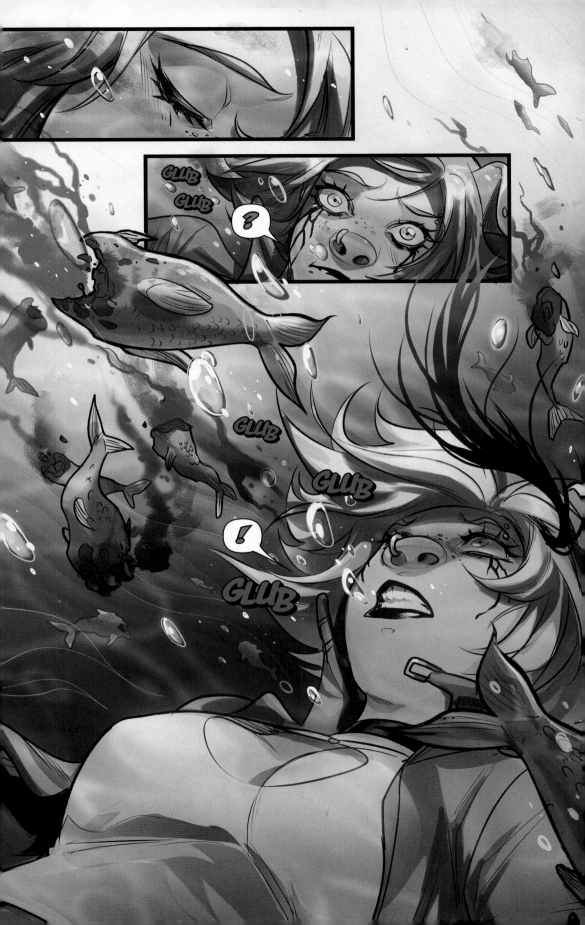

WHY AM I STILL ALIVE?!

BECAUSE YOU'RE STILL *FIGHTING*, LESLIE...

BECAUSE, DESPITE YOUR *ACTIONS*, YOU *DO* WANT TO SURVIVE THIS.

NO...THIS IS *NOT* GOOD. THIS IS *NOT* WHAT WAS SUPPOSED TO HAPPEN.

I CAN'T KEEP *DOING* THIS.

LESLIE!

KHAL! SAYA! GET *AWAY* FROM ME! THE *ALBINO*--HE'LL MAKE ME *HURT* YOU! *KILL* YOU!

HE'LL *TRY*, BUT AS LONG AS THERE'S STILL SOME OF *YOU* IN THAT BODY TO FIGHT HIM...HE'LL *FAIL*. WE'RE *SAFE* AS LONG AS YOU'RE--

UGH!
MY...MY HEAD!
OU IDIOTS!
YOU SHOULD'VE LISTENED TO MY BRIDE, SHOULD'VE RUN WHEN SHE COMMANDED IT.
NOW IT'S TOO LATE TO KILL US.
YOU TWO HAVE BEEN IN MY WAY FOR TOO LONG.
YOU ESPECIALLY, KHAL. DO YOU REMEMBER WHAT I TOLD YOU?
YOURS WILL BE THE FIRST LIFE I TAKE, BECAUSE...
B-BECAUSE...

AAAAARGH!
KHAL! I'M...
I'M SORRY...
PLOTCH
SAYA!
ABSURD!
MY BES...SHE STILL FIGHTS, STILL THINKS SHE HAS THE SLIGHTEST AMOUNT OF CONTROL...
SAVE YOUR TEARS, MY BELOVED WIFE.
THEY WILL NOT STOP ME.

L-LESLIE...
DON'T... DON'T LISTEN TO HIM. CRY IF YOU NEED TO, BECAUSE...
YOU'RE STRONGER THAN HE KNOWS... STRONGER THAN YOU THINK!
HE WON'T HURT US... YOU WON'T LET HIM...
UH?!
?
I KNOW. I'VE AWAYS KNOWN...
SAYA AND I BOTH HAVE FAITH IN YOU!

L-LESLIE...
EVERYTHING'S GOING TO BE OKAY.

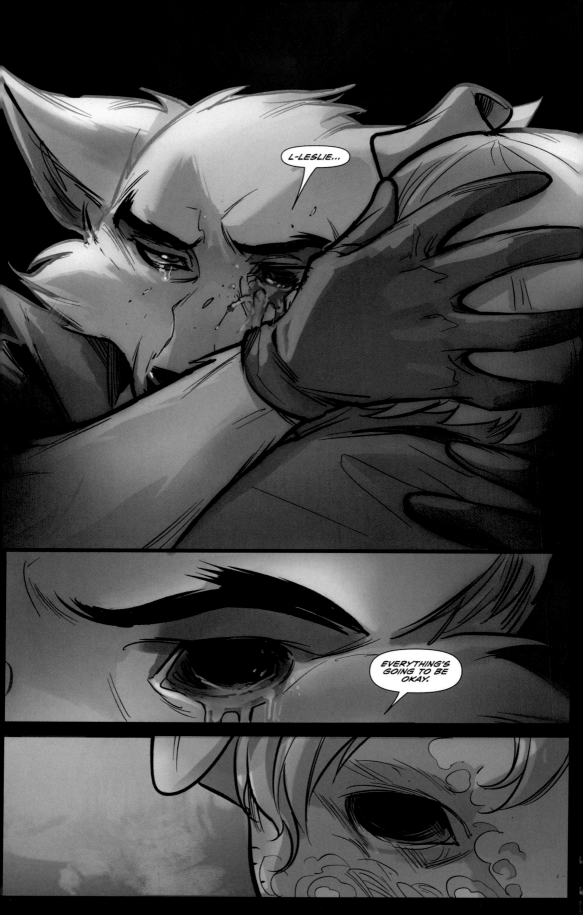

SPLAAASSH
UH?!
STOP PLAYING DUMB, CAROL. YOU THINK I LIKE HAVING TO WASH YOU? WOULDN'T HAVE TO IF YOU DIDN'T REEK!
SPLAAASSH
AAAH!
I SEE THE MEDICATION'S WORKING. I BET SOMEWHERE, DEEP DOWN IN YOUR PERVERT HEART... YOU'D LIKE TO GET UP, LIKE TO FIGHT BACK, BUT YOU CAN'T.
YOU CAN'T DO A DAMN THING TO ME.
WHEREAS I CAN DO WHATEVER I WANT TO YOU.
I COULD HURT YOU, PIG...
HELL, MAYBE YOU'D LIKE THAT?

MAYBE... I SHOULD USE THIS HOSE. I BET THERE'S A FEW NEW SENSATIONS I COULD SHOW YOU WITH IT.
BUT THEN, YOU DON'T LOOK LIKE SOMEONE WHO'S EVER HAD A MAN'S ATTENTION.
CRACK
DAMN IT! FUCKING BITCH!
YOU JUST WON YOURSELF A STRONGER DOSE!
THROOK
MORE DRUGS... AND MORE BRUISES, YOU DEGENERATE FILTH.
MAYBE AFTER THAT, FINALLY YOU'LL HAVE LEARNED TO BEHAVE.
!

Elsewhere.
IT'S ALL READY, GLANCE.
THANK YOU.
LEAVE ME.

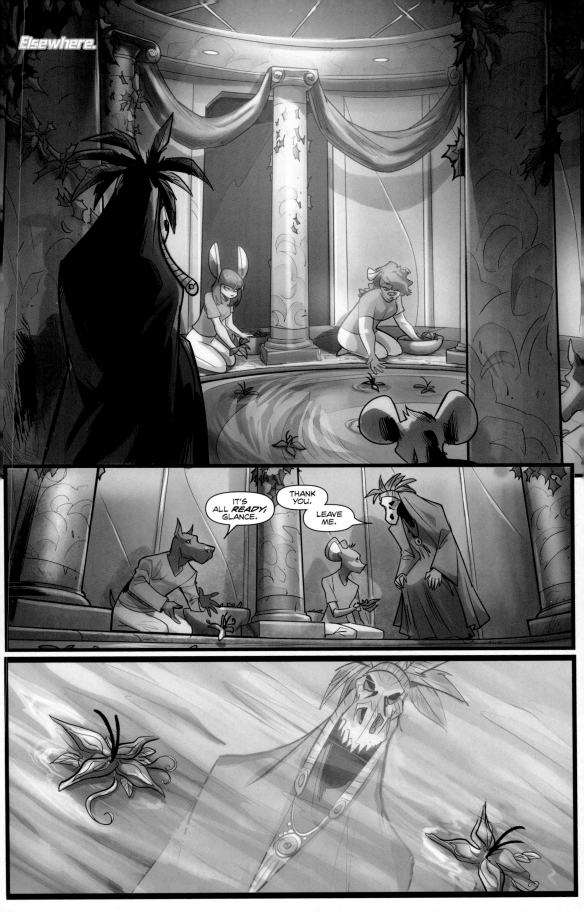

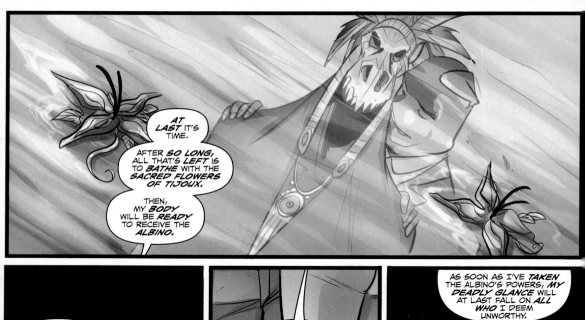

AT *LAST* IT'S TIME.

AFTER *SO LONG*, ALL THAT'S *LEFT* IS TO *BATHE* WITH THE *SACRED FLOWERS* OF *TIJOUX.*

THEN, MY *BODY* WILL BE *READY* TO RECEIVE THE *ALBINO.*

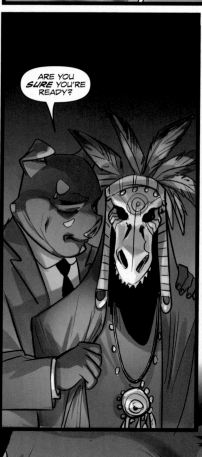

ARE YOU *SURE* YOU'RE READY?

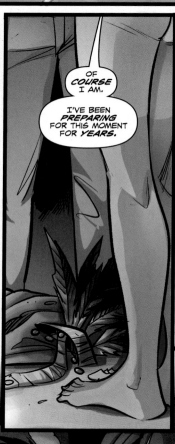

OF *COURSE* I AM.

I'VE BEEN *PREPARING* FOR THIS MOMENT FOR *YEARS.*

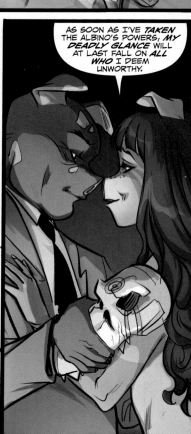

AS SOON AS I'VE *TAKEN* THE ALBINO'S POWERS, MY *DEADLY GLANCE* WILL AT LAST FALL ON *ALL WHO* I DEEM UNWORTHY.

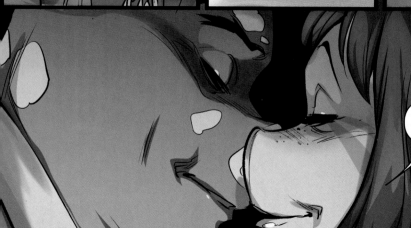

AND AT THAT *MOMENT...* THE NEW *PERFECT* WORLD WILL BE *BORN.*

THE WORLD WE'VE ALWAYS *DREAMT* OF... THE WORLD WE *DESERVE.*

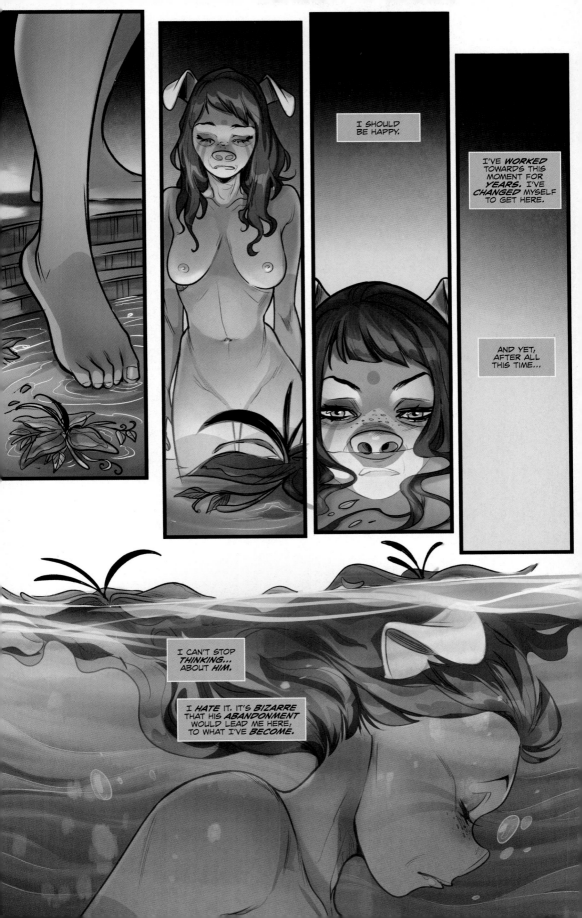

I SHOULD BE HAPPY.

I'VE **WORKED** TOWARDS THIS MOMENT FOR **YEARS**. I'VE **CHANGED** MYSELF TO GET HERE.

AND YET, AFTER ALL THIS TIME...

I CAN'T STOP *THINKING*... ABOUT *HIM*.

I *HATE* IT. IT'S *BIZARRE* THAT HIS *ABANDONMENT* WOULD LEAD ME HERE, TO WHAT I'VE *BECOME*.

WE'D BEEN CARRYING ON OUR UNHEALTHY, ILLEGAL RELATIONSHIP FOR SOME TIME...
IT WAS ONLY A MATTER OF TIME BEFORE THEY DISCOVERED US, BEFORE THEY SENT US TO JAIL.
BUT I DIDN'T CARE. I WAS DEEPLY IN LOVE...
AND EVERYTHING SEEMED RIGHT.
WHAT IF WE JUST LEFT? JUST YOU AND ME?
ANYTHING YOU WANT, MY LOVE.
I'D PAY ANY PRICE TO BUILD A LIFE WITH YOU.
I DIDN'T UNDERSTAND THEN JUST HOW WRONG IT ALL WAS.
WE WERE PERVERTING NATURE!

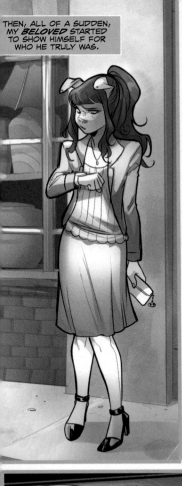

THEN, ALL OF A SUDDEN, MY *BELOVED* STARTED TO SHOW HIMSELF FOR WHO HE TRULY WAS.

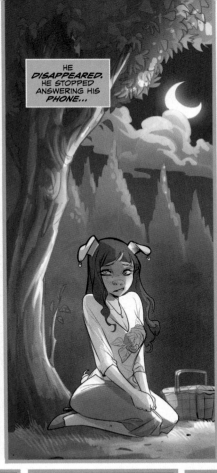

HE *DISAPPEARED.* HE STOPPED ANSWERING HIS *PHONE...*

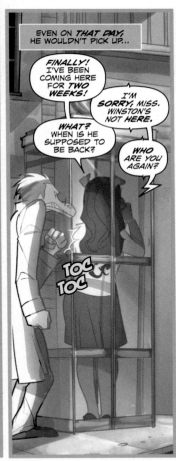

EVEN ON *THAT DAY,* HE WOULDN'T PICK UP...

FINALLY! I'VE BEEN COMING HERE FOR *TWO WEEKS!*

I'M *SORRY,* MISS. WINSTON'S NOT *HERE.*

WHAT? WHEN IS HE SUPPOSED TO BE BACK?

WHO ARE YOU *AGAIN?*

TOC TOC

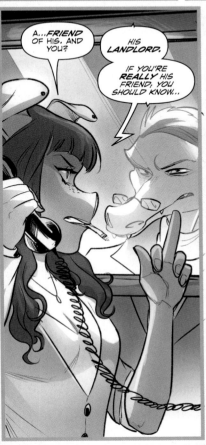

A...*FRIEND* OF HIS. AND YOU?

HIS LANDLORD.

IF YOU'RE *REALLY* HIS FRIEND, YOU SHOULD KNOW...

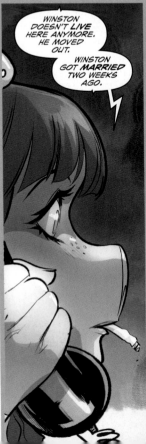

WINSTON DOESN'T *LIVE* HERE ANYMORE. HE MOVED OUT.

WINSTON GOT *MARRIED* TWO WEEKS AGO.

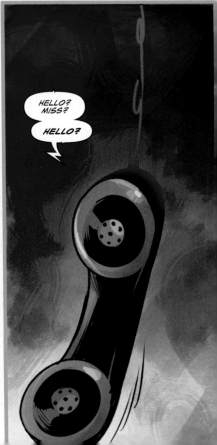

HELLO? MISS?

HELLO?

LESLIE! EAT YOUR DINNER BEFORE IT GETS COLD.
WHAT? IT'S YOUR FAVORITE!
SORRY, DADDY... I'M NOT HUNGRY.
I KNOW... BUT I CAN'T EAT WHEN MOMMY'S SAD.
?
OH, I'M SORRY, BABY... I JUST...
I DON'T FEEL GOOD. I THINK I NEED TO LIE DOWN.
GO TO YOUR ROOM, LESLIE...
DAAAD!
I SAID GO!
MAXIME!
WHAT'S WRONG WITH YOU? YOU'VE BEEN LIKE THIS FOR DAYS!
IT'S AFFECTING OUR CHILD!
YOU'RE HURTING ME.
ANSWER ME!
SCIAFF
DON'T TOUCH ME!
I CAN'T STAY HERE ANYMORE!
I CAN'T PRETEND TO BE HAPPY ANYMORE!

THEN GO! GO FUCK YOUR LION SOME MORE! YOU THINK I DON'T KNOW?
GO AHEAD, BITCH! ABANDON YOUR DAUGHTER!
AND DON'T BOTHER TO FUCKING COME BACK!
AND I DIDN'T BOTHER.
LESLIE WOULD BE FINE WITH HIM. HE HAD A JOB. HE WAS SECURE. I WASN'T.
I WANTED TO BE IN LOVE WITH PHIL, I DID.
BUT WINSTON... HE CHANGED ME, CORRUPTED ME...
THAT LION BASTARD RUINED MY LIFE.
EXCUSE ME...BUT ARE YOU OKAY, MA'AM?
WHAT'S WRONG? YOU'RE SHAKING!
HERE, IT'S OKAY... LET ME HELP YOU.

FUCK! YOU HAVE TO-- FUCKING DAMN IT!
GET OUT OF THERE! HURRY!
CAROL'S ESCAPED!
"WE NEED TO FIND HER. NOW!"
YOU IDIOTS!
LESLIE MAY BE ABLE TO PROTECT YOU FROM MY MENTAL ABILITIES...
BUT I STILL HAVE THE PHYSICAL STRENGTH OF A GOD.
YOU'RE JUST FLESHY PINCUSHIONS! THERE IS NOTHING YOU MORTALS CAN DO TO HURT ME!
THAT GOES FOR YOU, TOO, WOLFY...
IN YOUR CURRENT WOUNDED CONDITION, AT LEAST.
FOR-FORGIVE ME, LESLIE...
THERE'S NO OTHER WAY!
SLATCH
AAAH

GRRRR
STUPID BEAST...YOU ACTUALLY MANAGED TO SCRATCH ME.
THAT'S EARNED YOU A QUICK DEATH...
CAII
BUT NOT A PAINLESS ONE.
RUN, SAYA!
GET OFF ME, PIF!
THUMP
UGH!
I'M NOT DYING WITHOUT A FIGHT, ALBINO! I'LL STOP YOU...
EVEN IF IT KILLS ME!
TROOK
YOU'RE RIGHT ABOUT ONE THING...
FACING ME WILL BE THE LAST CHAPTER OF YOUR MISERABLE LIFE!
STOOMH

ALBINO?
DON'T. FUCKING.
MOVE.
?
THAT'S RIGHT. I TOOK A LITTLE SOUVENIR FROM THAT OLD FOOL'S HOUSE.
AND IF I UNDERSTOOD HIM RIGHT... THIS BLADE CAN KILL YOU, CAN'T IT?
STUMP
A BLADE IS ONLY AS STRONG AS ITS WIELDER...
...
ENOUGH. GHH IT'S OVER!
JUST LEAVE LESLIE ALONE!
NOW, ALBINO!
!

DO IT, KHAL...
DO IT! BEFORE HE TAKES CONTROL OF ME AGAIN!
YOU HAVE TO DO IT, KHAL. YOU KNOW YOU DO.
CAROL'S PLAN HAS FAILED.
NO!
EVEN IF CAROL'S PLAN FAILED, THERE HAS TO BE ANOTHER WAY!
THERE JUST HAS TO BE!
KHAL...YOU'RE LOSING MORE AND MORE BLOOD BY THE MINUTE. IF THE ALBINO COMES BACK, THE BEST WE COULD HOPE FOR IS KILLING EACH OTHER.
AT WORST, HE'LL KILL YOU BOTH AND THERE'LL BE NO ONE TO STOP HIM.
DO IT. DO IT FOR ME. THEN RESCUE CAROL AND SAVE YOUR SISTER.
PURRR
THIS HAS TO HAPPEN.
AT LEAST IF IT'S YOU DOING IT, I'LL DIE IN PEACE.
I-I...

GRAAAAWW
IF... IF THIS IS REALLY WHAT YOU WANT, LESLIE...
GRAAAAWW
UH?!
ZAC
AAARGH!
SKNIIIITC
PIF!
NOOOOOO!

CHAPTER
ELEVEN

On the Run.
...
LESLIE, I...I'M SORRY...
I DIDN'T MEAN TO.
I--I KNOW, KHAL...IT'S NOT YOUR FAULT.
PIF JUST ATTACKED. HE THOUGHT HE WAS DEFENDING ME...
THAT WAS THE LAST THING. EVERYTHING THAT HELD ME TO MY OLD LIFE IS GONE NOW...FOREVER.
AND I'M TIRED, I'M JUST...I'M REALLY TIRED.
THIS WHOLE NIGHTMARE, ALL THESE DEAD, RIGHT FROM THE BEGINNING...IT'S BEEN YOUR FAULT, YOU BASTARD!
DO YOU NOT SEE, MY BRIDE?
YOU'RE THE ONLY THING STANDING BETWEEN YOURSELF AND SALVATION, NOT ME.
I CAN STOP YOUR SUFFERING, PROTECT YOU FOREVER.
...NO.

I'M DONE LISTENING TO YOU, ALBINO! EVERYTHING YOU SAY IS BULLSHIT, YOU CONTROLLING FUCKING MANIAC!
YOU-- YOU STILL THINK YOU CAN RESIST ME?
YOU CAN TRY!
GNAK
AH!
I WILL, ASSHOLE. AND THIS TIME...
I'LL DO MORE THAN RESIST!

New Roark.
"HE--HELP! HELP ME!"
CRD
WHAT?! WHAT THE HELL HAPPENED HERE?
CAROL... THAT BITCH! SHE HIT ME WITH THE TABLET WHEN I WASN'T LOOKING!
IT'S DESTROYED! WITHOUT THE TABLET...
WE CAN'T TRACK CAROL! WE CAN'T SHOCK HER NERVOUS SYSTEM!
SHE SHOULD'VE BEEN UNDER HEAVY SEDATION...
APPARENTLY NOT... WHAT ARE YOU WAITING FOR?
FIND HER!
SPLIT UP.
LET'S GO.
NOW WHERE ARE YOU, YOU DEGENERATE PIECE OF--
SDONG

ALL THESE CELLS... THEY MUST KEEP THE CHILDREN HERE SOMEWHERE. POOR SHEA...
I CAN'T LEAVE HER HERE A SECOND LONGER.
UH?
GRRR
...
NO ONE SHOULD HAVE TO GO THROUGH THIS.
WHAT THE HELL ARE THEY DOING TO THEM?
AAAAH!
!

I'LL TEACH YOU SOME RESPECT, FATASS!
CIAFF
STOP!
WHO THE FUCK ARE YOU?
THAT'S NOT YOUR CONCERN, SHITMONGER!
SHEA! YOU NEED TO COME WITH ME.
DO--DO I KNOW YOU?
I'M CAROL.
YOU'RE TOO YOUNG TO REMEMBER, BUT I'M A FRIEND OF YOUR BROTHER'S...
AND WE NEED TO GO.
YOU'RE NOT GOING ANYWHERE, PIG!
I'M THE ONE WITH THE GUN AND SOMEWHERE TO BE.
MOVE!
FIRE, THEN!
FIRST!
OR DON'T. WE CAN ALL WAIT FOR SECURITY WHILE I HOLD ON TO THIS FAT LITTLE PANDA SHIELD.
DON'T DO IT, CAROL...DON'T SHOOT.

I CAN'T EVEN IMAGINE HOW YOUR TEACHER'S MADE YOU SUFFER.
TO THINK, HE'S ONLY ONE PERSON... AND THERE ARE SO MANY OF YOU.
YOU THINK YOU CAN TURN THEM AGAINST ME, YOU--
SGNACC
ARGH! INBRED FUCKING BASTARD!
SHE DIDN'T NEED TO TURN US AGAINST YOU! WE ALREADY HATE YOU!
YOU'RE THE MONSTER, NOT MY MOM!
GET OFF ME!
WE'LL COME BACK FOR THEM. BUT RIGHT NOW, WE NEED TO--
DROP THE GUN. AND GIVE UP.
DON'T MAKE ME SHOOT THROUGH A CHILD TO CONVINCE YOU, CAROL.
YOU'RE REALLY DOING THIS? THREATENING A CUB, MAXIME?!
IT'S FUNNY. YOU'RE OUTRAGED NOW...BUT THIS WAS YOUR PLAN.
THE PLAN. THE ALLIANCE. "SOME ANIMALS ARE MORE EQUAL THAN OTHERS."
THAT WAS BEFORE I KNEW ABOUT THE EVIL WE WERE IN BED WITH.
WE WERE YOUNG AND STUPID. IT WAS INSANE...AND WRONG!
THE ONLY INSANE THING I SEE IS YOU, CAROL. YOU AND YOUR IMPUDENCE.

EEEEE
WHAT?!
EEEEEEE
?
THE OTHER CHILDREN?
EEEEEEE
RUMBLE
RUMBLE
OUT OF MY WAY, FOOLS!
OKAY, CAROL... WHERE THE HELL IS SHEA?
THERE'S STILL TIME, MAXIME. YOU HAVEN'T DONE IT YET. YOU COULD STILL LEAVE ALL THIS BEHIND...AND COME WITH ME.
I'VE GOT EVERYTHING I NEED IN LIFE RIGHT HERE, CAROL. AFTER ALL, YOU TAUGHT ME WHAT I NEED...

"REMEMBER?"
WELCOME TO THE ALLIANCE, MAXIME JULIA SMITH.
AFTER YEARS OF PREPARATION, YOU'RE FINALLY OUR ADEPT.
ALL THIS, THANKS TO THE GOOD NAPOLEON, WHO INTRODUCED YOU TO US YEARS AGO.
CLAP
CLAP
CLAP
CLAP
CLAP
CLAP

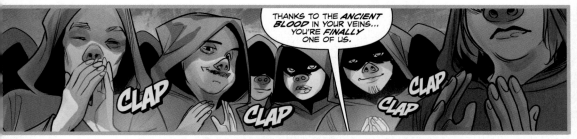

THANKS TO THE *ANCIENT BLOOD* IN YOUR VEINS... YOU'RE *FINALLY* ONE OF US.

CLAP CLAP CLAP CLAP

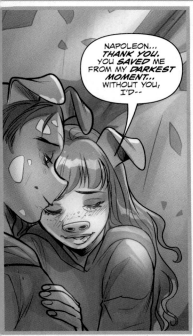

NAPOLEON... *THANK YOU.* YOU *SAVED* ME FROM MY *DARKEST MOMENT*... WITHOUT YOU, I'D--

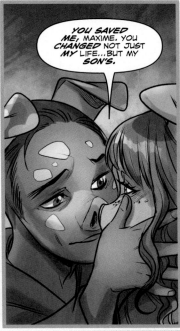

YOU SAVED ME, MAXIME. YOU *CHANGED* NOT JUST MY LIFE...BUT MY *SON'S.*

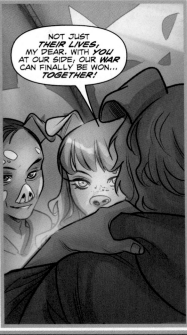

NOT JUST *THEIR LIVES*, MY DEAR. WITH *YOU* AT OUR SIDE, OUR *WAR* CAN FINALLY BE WON... *TOGETHER!*

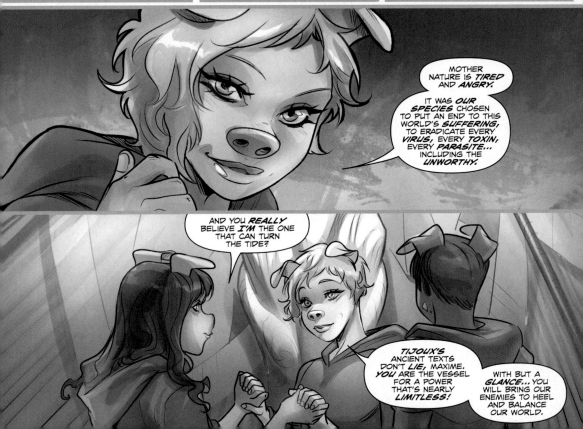

MOTHER NATURE IS *TIRED* AND *ANGRY.*

IT WAS *OUR SPECIES* CHOSEN TO PUT AN END TO THIS WORLD'S *SUFFERING*, TO ERADICATE EVERY *VIRUS*, EVERY *TOXIN*, EVERY *PARASITE*... INCLUDING THE *UNWORTHY.*

AND YOU *REALLY* BELIEVE *I'M* THE ONE THAT CAN TURN THE TIDE?

TIJOUX'S ANCIENT TEXTS DON'T *LIE*, MAXIME. *YOU* ARE THE VESSEL FOR A POWER THAT'S NEARLY *LIMITLESS!*

WITH BUT A *GLANCE*... YOU WILL BRING OUR ENEMIES TO HEEL AND BALANCE OUR WORLD.

THE SUIDE ALLIANCES HAVE LONG AWAITED YOUR COMING. FOR CENTURIES, WE'VE WIELDED POWER BEHIND THE SCENES OF THIS COUNTRY AND BEYOND. WE ARE BORN FOR THAT POWER, BORN TO LEAD.. THE ONLY ONES WORTHY OF IT!
OUR INTELLIGENCE IS SUPERIOR, OUR PHYSICAL STRENGTH DOMINANT, OUR WISDOM UNENDING. OTHER RACES EXIST TO SUBMIT TO OUR WILL. ANY AND EVERY ANOMALY THAT WOULD CHALLENGE THE PURITY OF OUR RACE MUST BE SUPPRESSED.
IT'S TIME TO GET OUT OF THE SHADOWS. FORCING THE DIFFERENT SPECIES TO SEPARATE IS ONLY THE BEGINNING. SOON IT'LL BE A FUTURE LINED WITH SEGREGATED GHETTOS. WE START BY BANNING INTERSPECIES RELATIONSHIPS, BUT SOON ANY INTERACTION AT ALL WILL BE BANNED.
PEOPLE ARE STUPID AND SCARED. THEY'LL BELIEVE ANYTHING. THEY THINK THEY'RE PROTECTING FUTURE GENERATIONS, WHEN THEY'VE NEVER NEEDED THAT PROTECTION. ALL WE WANT TO DO IS SEPARATE THE RIGHTEOUS FROM THE PROFANE...FROM THE DIFFERENT ONES.
ONCE WE'RE DONE, ONCE THE RACES ARE DIVIDED AND WEAKENED, THANKS TO YOUR DESTRUCTIVE POWER...IT WILL BE OUR SPECIES THAT DOMINATES.

ALL WE NEED TO DO IS ALLOW THIS POWER TO BECOME MANIFEST. AND FOR THAT, WE HAVE A VERY SPECIAL PLACE.
WE LEAVE SOON...
"FOR TIJOUX. ISOLATED FROM THE WORLD. THE BIRTHPLACE OF A LEGEND YOU YOURSELF BLINDLY BELIEVED.
"I UNDERSTAND. I TOO HAVE ALWAYS NEEDED SOMETHING TO BELIEVE IN.
"I WAS SKEPTICAL AT FIRST. BUT I BELIEVED NAPOLEON. I LOVED HIM.
"WHEN WE REACHED TIJOUX, WHERE SPIRITS WERE SUPPOSED TO BE FEARED AND VENERATED...
"I SAW A CHILD WITH INCREDIBLE STRENGTH, CLAWS LIKE DIAMOND, A DESCENDANT OF A CREATURE FROM FAIRY TALES. I FELT IT...THE ENERGY OF THAT PLACE SET FIRE TO MY VEINS.
"THE PEOPLE SEEMED SO TIMID. THEY WELCOMED US LIKE FAMILY.
"OF COURSE...THEY WOULDN'T HAVE, IF THEY'D KNOWN ABOUT OUR PLANS.

"WHEN THE SHAMAN SENSED BES'S LATENT POWER WITHIN ME, HE COULDN'T HELP HIMSELF. HE MADE ME HIS ASSISTANT. HE TRUSTED ME.
"EVEN WITH HIS FOOLISH TRUST...NOT EVERYTHING WAS GOING TO PLAN."
WHAT?!
DID YOU THINK SIMPLY BEING PART OF BES'S BLOODLINE WAS ENOUGH? YOU'RE NOT HER! YOU'LL NEVER BE HER.
IT DOESN'T WORK LIKE THAT. BECOMING A SHAMAN WON'T BE ENOUGH TO AWAKEN YOUR POWERS.
YOU MIGHT HAVE INHERITED SOME OF HER SPIRITUAL FORCE, BUT ONLY THOSE DESTINED TO TRULY BE BES CAN FULLY COMPLETE HER REINCARNATION.
READ THE PARCHMENTS. THEY DON'T LIE...YOU'RE TOO OLD. THE NEXT TRUE REINCARNATION OF BES MAY NOT HAVE BEEN BORN YET.
"I KNEW IT INSTANTLY, WHEN I SAW THE IMAGES IN THE BOOK, READ THE WORDS...SHE HAD BEEN BORN, AND I GAVE BIRTH TO HER.
"IT WAS THERE ON THE PAGE...BLUE HAIR, AND THE EXACT DATE OF LESLIE'S TWENTY-FIFTH BIRTHDAY."
YOU STILL HAVE VALUE. YOU'LL STILL BE A STRONG SHAMAN. YOU'LL LEAD THESE PEOPLE ONCE I'M DEAD.
THAT'S WHAT YOU WANT, ISN'T IT?
THIS IS A DISASTER!
IT--IT DOESN'T HAVE TO BE! WE CAN WAIT FOR YOUR DAUGHTE TO GROW UP! YOU'LL BE SHAMA THEN! YOU CAN AWAKEN THE ALBINO WITHIN HER AND TAKE THAT POWER FOR YOURSELF!
BUT ONLY IF YOU FOCUS ON THE FINAL TEST!
THE TEST THAT COULD KILL ME, CAROL? TRUST ME. IT'S ALWAYS ON MY MIND... THANKS.

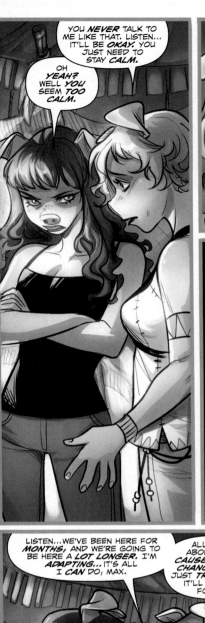

YOU *NEVER* TALK TO ME LIKE THAT. LISTEN... IT'LL BE *OKAY.* YOU JUST NEED TO STAY *CALM.*

OH *YEAH?* WELL *YOU* SEEM *TOO* CALM.

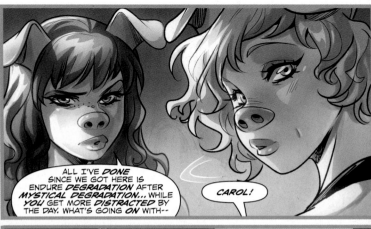

ALL I'VE *DONE* SINCE WE GOT HERE IS ENDURE *DEGRADATION* AFTER *MYSTICAL DEGRADATION...* WHILE *YOU* GET MORE *DISTRACTED* BY THE DAY. WHAT'S GOING *ON* WITH--

CAROL!

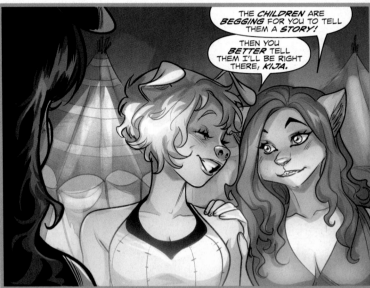

THE *CHILDREN* ARE *BEGGING* FOR YOU TO TELL THEM A *STORY!*

THEN YOU *BETTER* TELL THEM I'LL BE RIGHT THERE, *KIJA.*

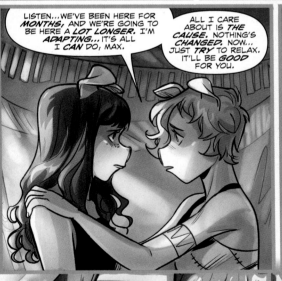

LISTEN...WE'VE BEEN HERE FOR *MONTHS,* AND WE'RE GOING TO BE HERE A *LOT LONGER.* I'M *ADAPTING...* IT'S ALL I *CAN* DO, MAX.

ALL I CARE ABOUT IS *THE CAUSE.* NOTHING'S *CHANGED.* NOW... JUST *TRY* TO RELAX. IT'LL BE *GOOD* FOR YOU.

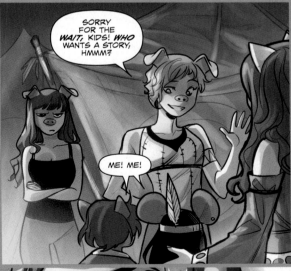

SORRY FOR THE *WAIT,* KIDS! WHO WANTS A STORY, HMMM?

ME! ME!

SCROOOSH

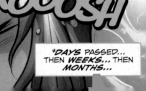

"*DAYS* PASSED... THEN *WEEKS...* THEN *MONTHS...*"

SCROOOSH
"BECOMING A SHAMAN DOESN'T HAPPEN SIMPLY OR QUICKLY...AT LEAST NOT IN TIJOUX. I HAD TO PURIFY MY BODY.
"IT WAS NECESSARY TO SAFELY ACCEPT THE COMING SPIRITUAL POWER. I HAD TO CONNECT TO NATURE, SPIRITS... AND THE LATENT POWER WITHIN MYSELF.
"I DID ALL THAT THINKING I'D SOON RAISE THE ALBINO AND ACQUIRE HIS POWER. I DID IT FOR THE CAUSE, CAROL! FOR YOU... AND NAPOLEON.
"YOU, HOWEVER... DIDN'T SEEM MUCH FOR SACRIFICE."
CAROL! DID YOU HEAR? NEXT WEEK I'M FINALLY GOING TO BE READY FOR THE FINAL TEST! FANTASTIC, RIGHT?
...CAROL?
"YOU WERE ALWAYS WITH THAT WOMAN AND HER UNWORTHY ANIMALS. RAIN OR SHINE, ALL THEY DID WAS DANCE! IT WAS ALL SO...
"UNBEARABLY HAPPY.

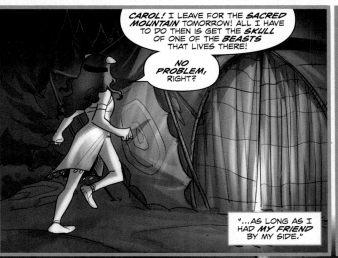

CAROL! I LEAVE FOR THE *SACRED MOUNTAIN* TOMORROW! ALL I HAVE TO DO THEN IS GET THE *SKULL* OF ONE OF THE *BEASTS* THAT LIVES THERE!

NO PROBLEM, RIGHT?

"...AS LONG AS I HAD *MY FRIEND* BY MY SIDE."

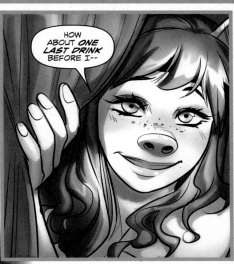

HOW ABOUT *ONE LAST DRINK* BEFORE I--

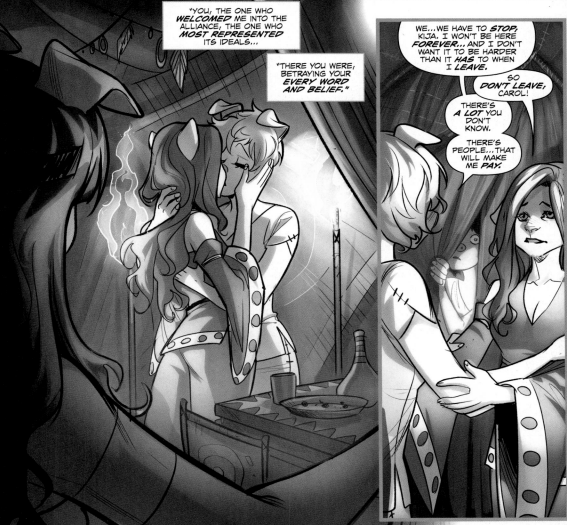

"YOU, THE ONE WHO *WELCOMED* ME INTO THE ALLIANCE; THE ONE WHO *MOST REPRESENTED* ITS IDEALS..."

"THERE YOU WERE, BETRAYING YOUR *EVERY WORD AND BELIEF.*"

WE...WE HAVE TO *STOP*, KIJA. I WON'T BE HERE *FOREVER*... AND I DON'T WANT IT TO BE HARDER THAN IT *HAS* TO WHEN I *LEAVE.*

SO *DON'T LEAVE*, CAROL!

THERE'S *A LOT* YOU DON'T KNOW.

THERE'S PEOPLE...THAT WILL MAKE ME *PAY.*

LET THEM TRY. I LOVE YOU, CAROL. AND YOU LOVE ME!
I'D PAY ANY PRICE TO BUILD A LIFE WITH YOU.
"THE WORDS WERE SO FAMILIAR.
"THE SAME STUPID LIES I'D HEARD BEFORE.
"TRUE LOVE WAS MEANINGLESS COMPARED TO THE PURITY OF OUR RACE!
"'I'D PAY ANY PRICE TO BUILD A LIFE WITH YOU.'
"ERADICATE ANOMALIES, SAFEGUARD THE SPECIES, SAVE THE ALLIANCE!
"THAT BITCH MADE YOU FORGET EVERYTHING! I COULDN'T ACCEPT THAT!"

?
URGH...!
IT'S OKAY, CAROL! SEE? SHE'S GONE!
SHE CAN'T DISTRACT YOU ANYMORE!
ARE YOU FUCKING CRAZY?!
AGH!
I WAS-- FUCK--I WAS FINALLY HAPPY!
IT'S NOT MY FAULT YOU LOST YOUR CHANCE FOR THAT!
THRUM
YOU'RE BEING RIDICULOUS, CAROL! SHE WASN'T ONE OF US!
CRASH

MY FUCKING EYE!
I--I DIDN'T WANT TO HURT YOU, CAROL! YOU WEREN'T THINKING, YOU ATTACKED ME! LET'S--LET'S JUST LEAVE, LET'S JUST GO HOME...
SLIIIP
AAAAAARGGH!

"IT WAS THE LAST TIME I SAW YOU...OR I *THOUGHT* IT WOULD BE.
"I DIDN'T GIVE A *SHIT* ABOUT YOUR DESTINY. AFTER WHAT YOU *DID*... I JUST WANTED TO FORGET YOU.
"YOU *GAVE* ME MY IDEALS, INSPIRED THEM...THEN *BETRAYED* THEM.
"A YEAR PASSED.
"MY *HATE* FOR YOU KEPT ME GOING...
"LONG ENOUGH TO *FINALLY* FIND THE *PERFECT VICTIM*... THE *PERFECT SHAMAN'S MASK*.

"IT WASN'T UNTIL I RECEIVED MY SACRED GARMENTS THAT I TRULY FELT LIKE I'D LEFT YOUR TREACHERY BEHIND, ALONG WITH THE REST OF THE PAIN FROM MY PAST LIFE.
"I WAS NO LONGER THE WEAK, BEATEN WIFE.
"I WAS NO LONGER THE SILLY, SEDUCED AND ABANDONED WOMAN.
"I WASN'T EVEN THE DEGENERATE MOTHER WHO BORE A DAUGHTER WITHOUT LOVE.
"NONE OF THOSE OLD MAXIMES REMAINED.
"THEY WERE DEAD, SACRIFICES IN TRIBUTE TO MY REBIRTH... AS THE GLANCE."
FORGIVE ME, CAROL.
YOU MUST BE BORED WITH THIS STORY BY NOW. YOU LIVED HALF OF IT.
PERHAPS WE SHOULD JUST GET ON WITH ITS BLOODY CLIMAX.
!
BAN--fssh
YOU WANT TO TALK ABOUT ENDINGS?
LET'S START WITH YOURS, MOM.
fssh

CHAPTER
TWELVE

CAROL PROBABLY DIDN'T TELL YOU ANYTHING, DID SHE? AND NOW...
NOW YOU KNOW EVERYTHING. SO MUCH FOR HER PROTECTING YOU FROM YOURSELF, LESLIE.
I'M NOT SOME FRAGILE PRINCESS. I DON'T NEED PROTECTION... NOT ANYMORE, AT LEAST.
NOT FROM YOU, AND NOT FROM ANYONE, GLANCE.
IN FACT, SPEAKING OF DANGEROUS...
"YOU SHOULDN'T HAVE LEFT US A HELICOPTER.
"THANKS FOR THE HELP, MOTHER."
AND... THE ALBINO? CAN YOU TRULY CONTROL HIM? IF SO...I'M PROUD, DAUGHTER.
AND IF SO... MAYBE IT'S TIME I TOOK OFF THIS MASK.
...
...WHAT?
HAVE I REALLY AGED THAT BADLY?

MY REFLEXES CERTAINLY HAVEN'T!
BANG
YOU WON'T HURT ONE MORE PERSON, MOTHER!
!
PTING
I'M COMING WITH YOU, LESLIE!
NO! STAY WITH SHEA.
YOU TAKE CARE OF THE PRISONERS WE FREED!
I LOVE YOU, SHEA. BUT I HAVE TO GO. LESLIE NEEDS MY HELP... YOU STAY WITH CAROL AND SAYA. I'LL BE BACK SOON... I PROMISE.
HELP LESLIE? YOU'RE HURT, KHAL!
IT DOESN'T MATTER. I'M STILL STRONG. I CAN STILL FIGHT. JUST KEEP AN EYE ON MY SISTER.
SAYA...DID YOU FIND BESS'S REMAINS?
NO, CAROL. ALL USELESS.
THAT MEANS...
LESLIE'S IN GRAVE DANGER!
IS SHE? I HONESTLY DON'T KNOW ANYMORE.
SHE WAS SO DIFFERENT WHEN SHE WOKE UP...